Tristan Hughes was born in Atikokan, around Llangoed, Ynys Môn, where he currently lives. He was educated at Ysgol David Hughes, Menai Bridge; the universities of York and Edinburgh, and King's College, Cambridge, where he completed a PhD thesis on Pacific and American literature. He is a winner of the Rhys Davies Short Story Award. *The Tower* is his first book.

The Tower

Tristan Hughes

Parthian
The Old Surgery
Napier Street
Cardigan
SA43 1ED
www.parthianbooks.co.uk

ISBN 1-902638-36-0

Typeset in Sabon by JT

Printed and bound by Dinefwr Press, Llandybïe

With support from the Parthian Collective

Editor: Gwen Davies

"Ley Lines" was first published in *New Welsh Review*.

Parthian is an independent publisher that works with the support
of the Welsh Books Council and the Arts Council of Wales.

A cataloguing record for this book is available from the British Library.

Cover Design: Jack Jackson
Cover Art: Peter Bodenham
Portrait Photography: Evan Hughes

For my mother and my father,
Patsy and Eifion Hughes

I would like to thank those various Ynys Môn clans who have, directly and indirectly, helped me with *The Tower*. Firstly and foremostly my own, the Hugheses, but also the Pollocks and the Morrises. And then some individuals: Big Dave, Hannah, and Sacha. I'd also like to thank all those from the back room of The Bull who, in the best ways possible, made sure this book took longer to write than it otherwise would have. And finally, Gwen Davies, whose deft editing and constant encouragement made sure it was finished more quickly than it otherwise would have been.

I pace upon the battlements and stare
On the foundations of a house, or where
Tree, like a sooty finger, starts from the earth;
And send imagination forth
Under the day's declining beam, and call
Images and memories
From ruin or from ancient trees,
For I would ask a question of them all.
    From "The Tower", WB Yeats

The Tower

God's Breath   1

Ley Lines   31

The Tower   53

The Importance of Being Elsewhere   73

Persistence   91

Of Rocks and Stones   115

Ynys   137

God's Breath

God's Breath

She is standing over by the sink, my nain, peering through the window with an old and antiquated pair of binoculars. They were given to my taid on the eve of his departure for the war in Burma, and he carried them with him through the entire course of that long and terrible excursion, and then back again to this kitchen, where they have sat ever since. If you were to look closely then you would see faint traces of this history scored upon their surface, slight scratches and abrasions that remember distant times and places. They have seen a great deal, these binoculars — armies, wars, continents, half of a whole century; more than I could ever imagine. But today the world crowded within their lenses is not so vast and populous: no more than a small patch of ground, a hill, the tower that sits upon it, and the piece of sky that hangs above them.

The view from my nain's window starts with the two fields in front of her farmhouse. They are her husband's fields. In the spring and early summer they are tall with grass and dotted with deliciously yellow buttercups. During the rest of the year they are sprinkled with Friesians and Limousins of all sorts of different shapes and sizes. The farmhouse is on a slight hill and both fields roll downwards from the doorstep towards a small lane that trickles along beside a little stream; together they go, hand in hand, until finally they meander out of sight towards the nearby sea. On the other side of this lane three more fields are visible and rise quite steeply upwards, making it look like a miniature valley. These fields all belong to Jack Cucu now, whose father grew up with my taid and went to the war with him. There is a slightly scruffy caravan in the corner of one of them; it belongs to two English hippies, a man and a woman, who my nain has quite a lot to say about. At the top of Cucu's fields an old stone wall reaches up steeply and above it sit the ruins of an old tower sticking out against the horizon, and behind which, on a clear day, you can see the edge of Snowdonia lurching down towards the sea. Far to the left, which from the window is the direction seaward, you can just about catch sight of a cottage that has been refurbished by its owner — a wealthy Scouser called Derrick — in a style that I can only describe as Texas Rancher Chic, and which has earned him, among us locals, the soubriquet Derrick Dallas. Dallas happens to be the owner of the ruined tower and for some time has been planning to restore it, or rebuild it in some way, and today he is standing beside it, along with a collection of architects and builders.

"Esgob Mawr!" she finally spits out. "What's that bloody Dallas up to now? I can see him up there with Jack Bach and Bobby. I don't recognise the other two. What in God's name does he want with that old tower — he can't leave anything alone, you know; no, he's always trying to build this and that, throwing his money around. But why would he want to start messing around with that old place?" Much of this is directed at the window, but I take the pause as my prompt to contribute my own thimbleful of local knowledge to aid in the explication of Dallas's designs. Even though my nain knows about *everything* around here, she occasionally allows me to offer up whatever measly trifles I have gleaned, just to make me feel better, just because I am her grandchild. Dallas, I say boldly, according to Jack Bach anyway, is planning to turn it into a kind of reception house, with circular bars and leather couches inside, and a viewing platform on the roof.

"Is that what they say then, is it? A fancy drinking place for his cronies and him, and a whole building just for that."

Secretly I am slightly proud to have fathomed so quickly Dallas's mysterious ways; but, just as I begin to bask in the extent of my own insight, my nain issues a subtle rebuke, one which insinuates that I have grasped at the shallowest and most obvious of explanations, that, like the greenhorn I am, I have merely dipped my toe into the deep ocean of men's motives. "Is that what they say then, is it. Well, I've known men like Derrick Dallas before, and they never build things just because they need them, or even want them for that matter — they build them because they can. It's always to show everyone that, at the drop of a hat, they can. These Sais moneybags, you know, they come here so they can play at being lord of the bloody manor; that's what they want to be: the lord of all they survey." At this point my nain turns haughtily away from the window and busies herself with buttering an ominously tall stack of bara brith, much of which it will soon be my duty to consume. In the distance I can hear the faint droning of my taid's tractor, wheezing its way through rutted fields. Otherwise, for a while, silence fills the kitchen. And then my nain begins to tell me a story about the tower. I do not know why it is this story, or why she chooses this moment to tell it, but somehow I think it is the invocation of Derrick Dallas's proprietorial gaze that provokes her; that it is her best reminder that whatever scope and breadth his money accords, there is much that lies beyond it. That however much Derrick's beady and accumulative eyes can possess, there are things that they can never see; a wealth and a richness that are hers, and hers alone to bequeath. She is giving me a gift that no Scouse Croesus could ever own, or confer.

****

Perhaps these days we have become accustomed to exotic beginnings and far-flung ancestries. Most people I know, when they talk about their progenitors, manage to unveil the most picturesque of characters, the most arduous, Odyssean of wanderings. There is usually a dissident shepherd from Kazakhstan, smuggled across the Urals beneath a faithful ram; a dainty, dashing Huguenot, who battled stormy seas with a glass of Beaujolais unspilt in his gloved hand; at the least a flamy-haired Irishman, fighting and gambling his way across continents, before inexplicably depositing his genes in Milton Keynes. Unfortunately, I have no such colourful relatives to hand. My nain was born in our village, which is about a mile and a half from where we are sitting in her kitchen. Nevertheless, her story begins with the one significant, if quite short, move in her life. My nain had eight sisters, which I'm sure today would be considered a rather wonderful thing, but in the middle of the 1930's, in a small Welsh village, was considered more of a headache. What was one to do with such a collection? The answer seemed to be to wait until they were sixteen or so and then spread them around, as generously as possible, amongst all those who were deficient in the way of daughters and such. If, for instance, providence had happened to gift you with a fine herd of milking cows and the lushest of pastures, but had also provided you with three hulking sons who where loath to soften their manly fingers by pulling teats of a morning, and a wife whose back was getting mighty sore, then — for merely the price of food and lodging and a shilling on Sunday — you could acquire one of my nain's sisters. Well, my nain had waited, with some trepidation, as year by year her bulwark of older sisters had been whittled away and dispersed across the island, until one fine spring day her father had returned from the local tavern, merry as a lord, and announced that he had found her a grand position, and not that far away either. She was to be sent, the very next week, to the household of the mighty euphonious-sounding Gruffydd Felin.

The road from the village to my nain's house is short and curved; if you looked at it from above, it would resemble the print of a horseshoe. In fact, here in my nain's kitchen, there is an aerial photograph — encased by glass and framed in brass — that would give you just such a view. Almost everyone around here has one. One day, many years ago, a mysterious plane came swooping down over this corner of the island and, for hours and hours, criss-crossed the sky above us. No-one knew what it was up to but conjecture ran rife for some time afterwards, mainly based around the theory that it was the agent of some kind of murky government espionage, perpetrated by the department of agriculture. During the days that followed there was a great hubbub as all the farmers rushed to conceal their unregistered animals, dig up planning permission for stray sheds and barns and in general push into the deeper shadows any traces of illicit husbandry. It was the cause of much relief then when a man suddenly started appearing on people's doorsteps, offering them the chance to buy aerial photographs of their homes, which, he assured everyone, had been the purpose of the plane all along. Well, they turned out to be extremely popular, these photographs — few self-respecting kitchens around here are without one — and allowed many a Welsh wife to look down upon her own house, when for years she had been restricted to looking down on those of her neighbours.

They have a slightly eerie quality for me; I am a little perturbed by the blank, uncomprehending omniscience of their gaze. Every inch of ground within their brass borders is as familiar to me as the back of my hand; I have stumbled over each snaking wall, fallen from each tree, trodden every blade of grass in every field; I have probably drunk tea and gorged myself on cakes in every kitchen. And yet, when I see these places glimpsed from above, captured on film by that entrepreneurial Icarus, they take on an alien quality — like Moonscapes or the Martian mountains — that I can't really explain. There they are — my taid's haybarn, Cucu's sheep pen, the old chapel and the fields that stretch into the sea — as clear and plain as day, but somehow they have been translated from actual things and places into flat, geometric spaces and planes, abstractions of colour and shape, Cubist dislocations.

A shift in perspective can be a dizzying experience: what I have known horizontally, as a sequence of glimpsed and moving horizons — tangled thickets of brambles and willow opening onto fields, tracks through small valleys rising upwards and disclosing vistas of rolling green — seems to have little to do with what I see vertically in these photographs. But it is more than just that. My ground level views were captured with mud on my shoes, with thorns in my hands, with nettle stings on my arms; for better or for worse I felt my way around this landscape, never knowing what would come next. These photographs, that claim to show you everything all at once, really show you nothing at all.

Anyway, after chapel on an April Sunday in 1935, my nain packed a small canvas bag with clothes and set off. Because it was not that far, she walked. It was the first really warm day of the year and by the time she reached the halfway point of her journey, where the horseshoe begins to curve upwards towards a gorse-capped hill called Y Marion, she had started to sweat, cursing her mother's decision that she wear her Sunday best — a dress of thick grey wool — in order to impress her new employer. That distant April sun proved a cruel and unrelenting adversary to my nain; its rays beat down through the unfurled leaf buds that hung in the trees along the road, creeping into the wool of her dress where their warmth was translated into an itchy, prickling heat. The further up the hill she got the harder they seemed to fall. The gorse bushes that topped Y Marion had just blossomed and their bright yellow flowers were spread above her like a furnace. But on she went, sweating and scratching, with dark wet patches all over her dress and her hair gone frizzy and so bloody hot that she couldn't even think of being nervous, until finally she reached a fork in the road that veered suddenly downwards. In front of her stretched pretty much the same view that, sixty odd years later lies outside her kitchen window, except that then her home was just another little stone cottage, its walls a glaring, starchy white in the brutal sunbeams, and which, for reasons of female modesty, she hoped nobody was looking out of (my taid still maintains that he was indeed looking out the window that day, and what a sight she was he says, he'd seen soldiers look better after a day's march through the jungle).

The other great difference was the tower. My nain is not a woman who is much given over to nostalgia, except in the most perfunctory, grandmotherly of fashions — vegetables have lost their flavour over the years; there'll never be another Nye Bevan — no, for her the past is comfortably the past, somewhere she inhabited and was happy to be, but not somewhere that she overly yearns to return to. Being an inordinately tidy and practical woman, she has gathered it up and stored it carefully away; her memories are like precious stones or Sunday silver, they are too valuable to leave strewn around in the everyday workings of consciousness. Nostalgia, in my nain's eyes, would be like wearing diamonds while you milked the cows, or serving chips on your best china. But when she describes that tower for me there is a certain and unmistakable hint of loss in her voice — almost astonishment — that time should have so diminished the object of her youthful gaze, that solid stone should prove so frail, that her own flesh and bones could have watched over its slow decline. And maybe that astonishment is partially mine too, because the tower that she delicately unpacks for me from where it has lain all these years is almost beyond what I can conjure up from the rubbly leftovers. It is a shadowy, spectral presence that, try as I might, I find hard to affix to the cold rocks that remain.

She says it was tall, maybe forty feet or more, and had a broad circular base from which it tapered upwards like a giant upside-down ice-cream cone. It was painted the brightest of white, which, on sunny days, shone with an almost luminescent quality, as though all the surrounding light was drawn towards it and condensed into its shimmering surfaces; set against the pale blue of a spring sky it flickered and dazzled like some inland lighthouse. But most striking of all were its four great sail arms. They were huge latticed wings, seventy feet from tip to tip, twisted at the end like propeller blades and fitted with canvas sailcloths. From afar they spun as silently and serenely as ghosts. Up close you could hear the slow whoosh of their massive revolutions, the air drawn away into their looping wake; you felt you might be uplifted with them, sucked into the gentle, momentary vacuum each swirling sail left behind in its passing. Standing beneath the tower and its sails it was as though there was nothing beyond its looming presence, as though it filled the whole horizon, the whole sky — its four great wings an airy constellation spread out across the heavens.

But on that faraway spring day, as she skulked past the cottage out of whose windows at that very moment, if we are to believe him, my taid was sardonically looking, it was another presence that preoccupied my nain's attention: a young sheepdog named Carlo. Carlo is the progenitor of many generations of snarling, yellow-eyed, canine misanthropes — all named Carlo —

who my family have loved and avoided over the years, and this ur-Carlo, apparently, had condensed within him enough genetic malevolence to supply his progeny for millennia to come. Maybe it was some presentiment that this flustered, heat-afflicted girl would one day be his owner that inspired Carlo to greet my nain with his characteristic welcoming gesture that day, but whatever his motivations were (the Carlos I've known have all worked in mysterious ways), the result was a dress that looked so shredded and torn that its wool might as well have just that moment been sheared from the sheep. At least, my nain says, she was better ventilated after his attentions. Anyhow, by the time she made it down past the cottage and to the foot of the opposite hill, on which the tower was perched, my nain was in a woeful state. Her dress a heap of rags, dripping with sweat and dog saliva; her face as red as a ripe tomato; her hair as dry and strawy and cowlicked as last year's scarecrow. And as the thought of meeting her new employer in such a dishevelled condition began to make her face burn still further, it suddenly occurred to her that her canvas bag contained pretty much all she needed to improve her situation: a change of clothes, a brush, and a little mirror.

Now it just so happens that at the bottom of that hill there is a copse of tall oaks. They arch over a stream and, in the spring and summer, create a cool and shady little glade which is as pretty and tranquil a place as you are likely to find in any real or mythological landscape. You can imagine then, my nain's relief when she slipped into this closeted nook. It being the end of April there was a soft carpet of bluebells on the ground, whose aching, beautiful blue was as sweet and refreshing as a fountain of ambrosia. Everything seemed perfect: the brook babbled, swallows twittered in the leafy rafters, there were even butterflies fluttering amongst the flowers. My nain could not have found a better natural boudoir in a Disney cartoon. Unfortunately though, her dress did not conform to the usual standards of silken, sylvan gracefulness of most heroines' costumes. It might have been the sweat drying in the wool, or perhaps some kind of Methodist prudishness sewn into the design (chapel dresses, I suppose, were not constructed with an eye to their easy removal), but my nain's dress clung to her so steadfastly that afternoon that it seemed her mother might well have spread it on with a trowel. After an interminable struggle she managed to dislodge her arms, only to find that she couldn't push it down past her hips; the harder she shoved the tighter each fold grasped hold of her, until she was reduced to rolling around on the flowers, flapping and heaving and yanking like some strait-jacketed lunatic. Well, a little while later my nain decided that if pushing wouldn't work then she'd have to give pulling a go. So she grasped hold of her tattered hems and lifted them over her head, only to find that this time it was her shoulders that riveted the dress upon her, and that now it had become a blindfold into the bargain. At this point one of the stately oaks decided to intervene in the struggle, placing himself squarely in her careering path and knocking her onto the ground. She lay there for some time, hopelessly swaddled in the coarse, spiderwebby wool, listening to the mocking babbling of the brook, until another noise began to form itself nearby. At first she thought it might just be the bump on her head, still echoing away in the corridors of her cerebellum, but as it came closer she began to recognise, with a chill rising up her spine, the unmistakable clumping of leather boots on grass. I would like, for the sake of my nain's dignity, to picture this scene as if it were some Ovidian tableau — a river nymph, or other dainty woodland divinity, caught unawares in a state of alluring, innocent dishabille by some passing hunter — but the truth is, that at this particular moment, my nain resembled nothing so much as a beleaguered, petty-coated mariner wrestling with an octopus that had fallen on his head. And it was while she was lying prone in precisely this state that she first heard the gentle, faintly melancholy, voice of Gruffydd Felin, saying, very considerately she thought, "Well, you must be the new girl, you wouldn't want a hand, would you now."

****

Many of the older members of my family, including my nain, have a penchant for providing their remembered selves with tremendous powers of divination and inference. Retrospect has an uncanny habit of transforming these youthful protagonists into so many sibyls and seers, and to make the world they inhabit quite remarkably awash with omens and auguries. Now this is not to say that, looking back, my august relatives picture themselves as particularly canny detective-types, as the possessors of an especially sharp logical faculty that allowed them to see the obscure causal relation of events, no, far from it. What they claim is that at such and such a moment, because of such and such they saw, they just *knew* that something was going to happen. Usually there is quite simply no connection whatsoever between the portent and the ensuing incident. Thus my great-uncle Idris has assured me, on more than one occasion, that he was sadly aware of his beloved Mair's demise, six months before it came to pass, because he'd witnessed Dai Bach's prize bull, Monty, falling off the edge of a cliff; while my auntie Delyth absolutely insists that, unlike so many other young girls, the news of Buddy Holly's plane crash came as no surprise to her, seeing that she'd witnessed two foxes fighting over a dead rabbit the year before. Wars, elections, exam results, the break-up of the Beatles, all of them, at some time or another, have been foreseen in the most unlikely of fashions by the doughty elders of my clan. I don't really know how much credence I put in these mysterious powers of prognostication — they only seem to crop up *after* the foretold event has happened — but since they are inextricably woven into the fabric of my family memory I am loath to ignore them. One thing, at least, is certain: they make listening to their stories a difficult and demanding exercise. Because you never really know whether some throwaway detail, some apparently trivial occurrence or digression in the narrative, is actually the key to it all; that lodged in the observance of two rooks on a telegraph pole, or a punctured tractor tyre, or an unseasonably warm day, is the stories' conclusion. I shall try not to encumber you with the vagaries of this particular ancestral tradition. But just so you know, and without going into details, it is at this point in my nain's story that, so she tells me, the outcome of her stay with Gruffydd Felin became known to her.

After the restoration of her dress my nain and Felin set off up the hill towards the tower. She says that that walk, and the rest of that day, was like being in slow motion; whether it was embarrassment, or nervousness, or just resignation in the face of both, the world seemed to inch past her like a slothful caterpillar. A small herd of dozing cattle was spread out in the lower field, and amongst them was a beautiful grey calf with the bluest of eyes. Felin pointed it out with a listless finger. The sound of Felin's boots clacking on the stone slabs of the track frightened a company of fledgling magpies hiding in a nearby blackthorn tree, and my nain listened as the sound of their clumsy, leaden flapping receded into the distance. A black and white farm cat lounged on a stone, lifting his head to take a languid glance at them as they went past. The tower loomed above them, appearing bigger with each slow step, every torpid sweep of its sails moving through air as thick as treacle. It felt like there might be no way out of those long minutes, that time itself might congeal and strand them forever in some endless, amber afternoon.

There was an old aga in Felin's kitchen, against the far wall, with two black pans bubbling away on top of it, and as he went over to inspect them she looked at him properly for the first time. He was tall and thin, with stooping shoulders (only later, when she went inside the mill tower, would she understand the origin of that stoop) and wiry arms. His hair was as black as anthracite — though he must have been about fifty — but beneath it his face was a deathly, mortuary white, as though his skin had been embalmed and powdered as before burial. They said it was the miller's lot, this paleness, that the flour became ingrained in their skin over years, the way coal dust did with miners, turning them grey; they said she should have seen his father before he died — as white as an albino. What she saw in Felin's eyes was a watery greenness, the colour of algae on the stones of mountain streams, that never seemed to be still but always at the point of dispersal and dissolution; it was as if the liquescent confines of his irises were struggling to contain some swirling, centrifugal substance. You couldn't really stare straight at them, they made you a little dizzy.

Felin was still fussing with his pans when the kitchen door opened and Rhiannon Felin, his wife, waddled into the room. My nain is often slightly less generous with her descriptions of women then she is with those of men. She has a wonderful gift for sharp, acerbic observation and mimicry, and her impressions of those unfortunate enough to fall under her critical ken are nothing short of ingenious. The most innocuous looking of old ladies, who at first glance you would think had absolutely nothing out of the ordinary about them, turn out — when refracted through her deliciously malicious eyes — to be a walking compendium of grotesque gestures, comic mannerisms and physical abnormalities. It is a cruel and ruthless talent, but unerringly accurate and always — if you're lucky enough not to be its object — terribly funny. Now poor Rhiannon Felin must be one of my nain's masterpieces and I only wish I could convey to you in some way her performance. But, unfortunately, I have not inherited her particular talents. And besides, unless you could actually *see* it, with your own eyes, you would miss its subtlety, its exuberant panache. It is a sad truth this: that so many of the precious things that are gifted to our sight remain unreproducible; passing shadows on our retinas, perished cells, a lost detritus of synaptic explosions. But if I cannot put my nain's version of Rhiannon before you, in all its wicked glory, I can at least unearth a little of what provoked it. They stood in the kitchen, the three of them, for several minutes before anyone spoke. It was Rhiannon who broke the silence, opening her blubbery lips to inquire of her husband, "Well, is this her then?" She made no effort to conceal the hostility in her voice, or, in fact, to turn her black, molish eyes towards the uncomfortable girl who was standing less than six feet away from her. Felin looked up from the pots, the animus in his wife's voice sending a resigned, weary grimace across his face, and replied, "Of course it is. I went down to collect her."

Rhiannon did not soften an inch, spitting out "Did you now." And then it was quiet again, the pots bubbling, Felin poking at them and looking embarrassed, Rhiannon standing as stiff as a plank. The reasons for this cold reception are beyond me; but maybe the sight of a sprightly sixteen year old girl with flushed cheeks, dishevelled hair and a tattered dress, standing in her kitchen with her husband, was not something Rhiannon was used to.

There was a picture that hung over the small wooden table in the kitchen. It was a depiction of the last supper, painted in sombre, Victorian purples and greens, and numerous shades of grey. Jesus, who appeared stern and sad, was breaking a piece of bread and the disciples were all looking at him, none of them saying a word. A huge, melancholy silence filled the picture; no-one had anything to say, there was nothing to say. As she looked at the picture my nain felt herself slipping into this wordless vacuum, imagined long speechless days, endless mute nights. She had never felt this lonely in her whole life, and as she turned her gaze towards Rhiannon's fat, pursed, ungenerous mouth a hatred was conceived that would last, unabated, for over half a century. It is as keen and sharp today in this kitchen as it was all that time ago in that other one; the years have not diminished it, Rhiannon's death has not vanquished it, only my nain's demise will extinguish it — but I am not certain, even of that.

During the weeks that followed her inauspicious arrival my nain settled into a round of daily chores and duties. In the morning she would get up to milk Felin's five cows who, after a few days, developed a great affection for their new keeper, and would wait patiently for her by the gates to the shed, greeting her each sunrise with a soft chorus of friendly lowing. Then, after breakfast, she would go help Felin unfurl the canvas sailcloths. This was her favourite job. Each time it felt like an embarkation. The four tall sails would sit quietly and still in the early morning light, set at a slight angle like a skewed crucifix, before Felin wheeled them around and stretched out their canvas coverings. Then came the best part. The sails were fixed to a big, wooden dome on the top of the tower; it was called the cap, but it looked more like an upside-down boat. A thick iron cross was attached to the bow of the boat and out of its four sides grew the sails; while around the back, on its stern, a wooden rudder jutted out, carrying behind it a huge iron wheel around which hung a long, thick chain that dangled all the way down to the ground. After Felin had finished spreading out the canvas, he would walk off a bit and begin a strange, fidgety kind of ritual. First he would shuffle around in one stuttering circle, holding his fingertips to the sky; then he would arch his neck over his stooped shoulders like a turtle and scan the treetops, before taking one final glance at his white shirts on the washingline. He would be ready then, because no matter how bewilderingly the wind moved, or if it were as slight as a cat's tongue, Felin could always, often uncannily, fathom its direction. What with his shape and his skills they should have just stuck him on a weather vane, my nain says. And when he was ready he would walk over to the dangling chain and haul down on it. Each pull on the chain rotated the wheel, which in turn moved the whole boat around, sails and all. He would do this until the sails faced full into the wind and then, together, they would wait. It never took long, and there was always a feeling of the miraculous about it.

Out of nothing so it seemed, out of an empty, immobile morning, would materialise the first slow movements: the billowing of the narrow canvas; the gentle, anticipatory stiffening of the broad wooden blades; the slow straightening of the iron cross. And then, in the time it took to exhale a single breath, the sails took flight. To begin with they would arc leisurely up into the sky as though slightly sluggish and leaden after the night's long stillness, like a snake shuffling out of its winter skin and stretching itself out in the sun. But with each new turn they gathered a swifter momentum, swooping in and out of the sky until they had found the day's invisible rhythm and held it there, beating on the horizon. Standing below you could feel their motion eddying into the air. The day had come alive, its pulse was flowing all around you. In all the time she knew him these were the only moments my nain can remember when Felin smiled.

The rest of her day was usually an anti-climax. Sometimes she would roast oats in a small stone shed outside the Felins' house. It was a dull and uncomfortable job. The spring continued to be hot and, with the added heat of the kiln inside, the shed would become unbearable. But at least the stifling precincts of the kiln shed were preferable to the antarctic chill of the dairy, where Rhiannon exuded enough frostiness to make everyday a dark December one. She would sit there on a tall, creaking, wooden stool, watching as my nain churned butter wondering would it turn out as ice-cream. Rhiannon barely spoke more than five words to her over those first few weeks. Even when the two of them were forced into an uncomfortable proximity, usually at mealtimes, Rhiannon would maintain an attitude of sulky indifference, as though the girl in front of her might turn out to be some unwelcome optical illusion that if she kept ignoring, might eventually disappear. And yet, despite her aversion to my nain's presence, Rhiannon proved to be an almost ubiquitous companion; everywhere she turned, it seemed, there Rhiannon would be, appearing out of the corner of her eye like a portly apparition. At first my nain put this down to some kind of over-zealous supervisory instinct, Rhiannon making sure her new charge didn't upset the finely honed equilibrium of the Felin household. But it soon became apparent that her surveillance extended well beyond the confines of the house.

Most afternoons my nain had a couple of hours to herself and, because it was so close, she usually spent them beside the sea. It was a beautiful walk, down along a narrow lane surrounded by thick and luxurious hedgerows, heavy with the scent of honeysuckle and wild roses. The lane took you to the very edge of the cliffs, below which were two stony beaches separated by an outcrop of grass-covered earth and stone that jutted out into the sea like a fat knuckle. There were hidden paths (today the National Trust have turned them into veritable highways) that spidered down the cliffsides, through brambles and bracken, to the wedges of bright white stone beneath. Once there you were cloistered on all sides by cliffs and headlands, and the sea stretched out before you like it was your own. My nain loved to just sit there, watching seagulls hover and cormorants wink in and out of the water, picking through the stones which sometimes had strange fossil shapes on their sides, listening to the quiet rumbling sound the waves made as they dragged at the rocky shore. But even these moments of seclusion and solitude would be interrupted by a black shadow taking shape on the cliffs above, a malignant, squat silhouette set against a background of tranquil green. It never came closer, but lingered just long enough to eclipse all the beauty of a sunny, solitary afternoon.

It is strange how jealousy, once provoked, cleaves so closely to the objects that inspire it. Rhiannon, who I'm sure would have liked nothing better than to have never set eyes on my nain again, could simply not take them off her. What an odd couple they must have made, my nain and Rhiannon: a young and headstrong girl, who I'm sure even then was every bit the sharp-tongued chatterbox she is now, and the sullen, taciturn, middle-aged woman. That girl is unforgiving still of those unwonted attentions and the inexplicable suspicions that inspired them — what would I've wanted with an old man like Felin, she says, especially when your taid was living next door, more or less — but I'm not so sure Rhiannon was used to strong passions and the helpless delusions they arouse. No-one sees clearly in their hold and so how could Rhiannon, who had lived quietly and placidly and without even a quickening of her heartbeat I suspect, for the past twenty-five years, have been expected to understand the vivid distortions that crept into her sight that spring. The eye is not a looking-glass, after all, but a hall of crazy mirrors where our best and worst selves frolic amidst their own grotesque reflections. And besides, as the weeks wore on, and spring became summer, Rhiannon's was not the only peculiar behaviour my nain had to witness: there was something increasingly odd about Felin too. Looking back it seems to make sense, but hindsight is a fine thing isn't it.

****

There was no one event that you could have pinpointed and held up as definitive proof that Felin was becoming a little strange, no outlandish action or bedlamite outburst. He was an excessively quiet and gentle man, deliberate and careful too. And while men often go out of their minds, they seldom go out of their characters. No, there was no single occurrence but instead a series of gradual disturbances in his behaviour, riffles across the placid surface of his daily life that slowly grew into waves. At first my nain didn't even notice them. For instance, sometimes in the morning he would stand watching the tower's sails for just a few more minutes than he usually did, and without smiling either. Other times she would find him hunched behind the grain shed, smoking cigarettes when he should have been unloading the grain sacks. And as often as not there were only the tiniest inversions in his normal reactions and habits to provide clues that something might be amiss: a frantic laugh when usually there would have been silence; one egg in the morning instead of two. They were such small and imperceptible things that perhaps she wouldn't have noticed them at all if they hadn't been refracted and magnified through Rhiannon's suspicious eyes. Each night as they sat down for their normally intolerably silent supper, Rhiannon would startle everyone with pointed, accusing questions: "You were lingering around the kiln shed today, Gruffydd, is there something wrong with it?" "Well, there must be something almighty special about the tower these days, the way you kept mooning at it all morning." These questions became an agonising nightly ritual. Rhiannon would spit them out and Felin would sit there, looking for all the world as if he didn't hear them. And maybe he didn't. He looked old and lost those nights, more than he did in the daytime, my nain says, as though no sound — even Rhiannon's venomous outbursts — could reach him. It was like he'd receded into some unfathomable inner space and left behind a white and fleshy shell. There was a terrible, surreal quality to those nights: Rhiannon sitting at the table accusing a man of harbouring errant passions who at that moment looked as though he had forgotten all passion. It was like someone berating a marionette for its adulteries.

Felin was a man of few words. He'd been like that from the time my nain first met him that afternoon, and she had no reason to believe that he'd ever been otherwise; there was little to suggest that he'd declined from earlier, garrulous glories, that the words had dried up after some youthful monsoon. He appeared to be a naturally quiet man and to have always been one. At first this muteness, combined with Rhiannon's, had been painfully disconcerting for my nain, who had grown up among a throng of babbling sisters and was used to living amid endless, frenetic conversations. But she had quickly learnt that silence had its own frequencies and textures, and to distinguish between Rhiannon's sharp, bitter taciturnity and Felin's soft wordlessness. She liked him. His lack of speech seemed a part of his innate delicacy, his calmness. Words were a turbulence to be kept to a minimum; they were uncertain winds. So perhaps it isn't surprising that the most striking evidence that something was wrong with him was the day he engaged my nain in a conversation, or, to be strictly accurate, the day he spoke more than two sentences to her.

It was such a startling occurrence that she remembers quite clearly its circumstances. It was a hot, cloudless afternoon, around the middle of July, and she was just about to set off towards the beach. By this time she had got into the habit of making a quick reconnoitre of her surroundings before she embarked, on the off-chance she might glimpse Rhiannon following her. Well, straight away she'd sensed some subtle distortion in the scene around her, though it took her a good while to locate what it actually was. The sails on the tower were still. Now Felin always worked the mill right through the afternoon, however light the wind, and my nain had become so used to the motion of the sails during this time of the day that it had become an almost natural phenomenon to her; if she'd walked out that afternoon and found all the oaks at the bottom of the field covered in a foliage of vivid purple, or looked up and seen the sun wheeling eastwards across the sky, she would've barely been more surprised. At first she thought it might be some trick of the light and blinked a few times to make sure, but no, there they were, absolutely stationary. It took her a few more seconds to register the steady, balmy breeze blowing directly into her face. The day suddenly felt all out of kilter, a scattered jigsaw picture, and instead of heading down the lane towards the sea my nain walked up towards the tower. It was empty when she got there.

On the other side of the hill, opposite the side that looks across at my nain's house, a series of wide, undulating fields stretch out towards the shore and beyond to an ancient, holy island named after a saint, or a bird — whichever you prefer. If you walk about three hundred yards down from the tower in this direction you'll come to an old stonewall, in the middle of which two loving sycamores have grown up hopelessly entwined. The result of their lengthy embrace is a rather neat frame of branches, the shape of church windows, with the island nestled right there in the centre. Now I don't pretend to know how this works, although I'm sure it's a very simple case of framing and perspective, but if you walk directly towards the trees and keep your eyes on the island it actually shrinks the closer you get. I remember the first time I saw this, as a young boy of around eight or nine. I was walking with my taid and he told me to look right at the island through the branches and tell him what I saw. It took a while, but when I noticed the island slowly contract I was baffled and amazed — I thought that it was some miraculous adult trick, something that my taid had conjured up for my amusement. At the time he never let on that it might be otherwise. It was towards this very spot that my nain headed on that July day, for no other reason, I suppose, than that her day had already been tilted from its ordinary course by the frozen sails. And it was right between those trees — younger and leaner back then, but already in a state of advanced flirtation — on that same wall — already old, even then — that she found Felin sitting. And, to tell the truth, he did look a bit smaller than usual, or so my nain tells me.

It was a while before he noticed her. She was standing about ten yards away, half thinking of sneaking away, when he turned his swirling green eyes towards her. The skin on his face was like cold, melted wax. For a while he just looked at her, a vertiginous stare that made her feel unsteady on her feet. She tried to focus on the island behind him. And then he began to speak in a low murmur and it was the strangest speech she had ever heard.

"I'm sorry," he said, "but I've not got the heart to keep them going today. I know I should but I can't and I don't think I will ever be able to again. My whole life I've worked with the air, nothing but the air, and I know I'm not that much use these days. I'm not stupid, I know there's better ways these days. But it's all I've ever done. I make things out of God's breath. I don't kill things, I don't dig things up or break them down, I don't steal things, I don't do anything that hurts anyone. And when I watch them now all I can think of is that when I'm gone and when they've gone there'll be nothing left because you can only see the wind when it moves things. And if I can't see his breath how will I see Him." And that was it. He turned his face away and left my nain standing there. After a while she walked away, thinking he'd gone a bit crazy and wondering what you were supposed to do when that happened. There'd been a few mad people in the village but nobody really did anything. They would just act around them like their craziness wasn't really there, like it was some froward child that was best ignored, and then when they'd gone they'd whisper together about how cucu they'd gone, poor thing. Besides, there seemed to be gradations of crazy in the village, and the ones who went good Methodist mad and talked a lot about God were usually considered the most harmless; pious loonies who had had one draught of divine afflatus to many — a venial sin in anyone's book. So, by the time she got back to the house, my nain had made up her mind that if Felin — who she liked and was gentle and quiet — was given over to the odd strange utterance, then that was his business.

Unfortunately, after that day, Felin, true to his unexpected words, put aside the life he'd lived for fifty years.

* * * *

It is not so hard, in a country where there are bwgans abounding — in every garden, at every cross-roads, behind every gravestone — for living men to join the company of their spectral neighbours. There is an amorphous boundary in this place between flesh and shadow and from time immemorial we have slipped, unwittingly, across it — through caves and river banks and groves of oak — and, as often as not, returned, blinking and befuddled. And so if I say that Felin became a living ghost after that afternoon, I don't mean it entirely as a metaphor. He was there corporeally, of course, but his spirit had receded into some faraway place, some dark backward abysm of the mind where the world must have flickered as weakly and distantly as starlight. Occasionally some evidence of this terrible hinterland would find its way to the surface: he would often start crying for no apparent reason, inexplicable tears that made their way from unfathomed, subterranean depths and glistened with an alien brightness on his white skin. It was awful, my nain says. There was nothing they could do. He would barely move during the day, except to haunt the empty fields down by the sea; a thin and stooping wraith framed by the ocean. At night he would sit at the kitchen table in the darkness, watched over by a silent, tenebrous Jesus and his mute disciples. Nothing they could say or do. He never spoke a word.

Rhiannon, who had spent all summer chasing shadows, decided she wasn't that happy living with one and went to stay with her mother in the village. My nain stayed. Not that she chose to, mind you, but because somewhere in the village it had been decided that Felin needed someone there to keep an eye on him. They needn't have bothered she says, she might as well have been in Timbuktu those last few weeks, for all the good her presence did him. You see the thing about keeping house for a ghost, she tells me, is that eventually you come to feel like one yourself. When she walked around the cottage and the outbuildings there was an overwhelming sense of abandonment, as though she had happened upon some deserted world where she no longer belonged, that existed already in some other dimension. And Felin himself seemed increasingly a part of this landscape, at one with its deserted, otherworldly spaces. In the end it was hard to distinguish who exactly was haunting whom.

She says it was the tower that made her feel most alone. Its motionlessness made the air seem empty around it. An aura of deathly enchantment surrounded it, which made her feel, whenever she approached it, as though she had fallen suddenly into the static realm of someone else's dream and could not get out. Its arrested sails, hanging on the horizon, were like the hands of a stopped clock in a symbolic house, signalling a new form and order of time. It was Felin's tower and had sunk with him into that other place.

Though it might be difficult to imagine, my nain says she wasn't at all surprised when she found Felin dead inside the tower. He was dangling from a long chain that was used to haul sacks of grain up into the top floor. Everything inside was perfectly neat and tidy; there was no sign at all that he had struggled much when dying. A thin powder of flour dust covered the stone floor and when she opened the door the breeze picked some of it up and swirled it into the air. Although this was the first dead person she'd ever seen, only one thing really shocked her when she looked up at Felin: the colour in his sightless eyes had stopped, dead still.

Ley Lines

We're in the middle of these lines, Skinner had told her the first night they'd met. He'd told her how they were magical lines, lines that marked the earth's secret, covert energies, ley lines. They're everywhere, he'd said, like veins under the skin, the world's hidden heartbeat pulsing through them. That was the first night Gemma had slept with him and afterwards she'd wondered if his speech about the lines had actually attracted her, or if the pills she'd taken had made her a bit in love with the first person to really talk to her and put their arm around her, or if maybe the mixture of MDMA and mysticism was a pretty damn potent aphrodisiac. In any case, during the days and weeks that had followed she'd realised that Skinner's geomancy was only a part of a much broader — if somewhat more vague — theory, that, after much attentive listening, she had deciphered as follows

Skinner believed that there was power everywhere, which, in strictly Manichean fashion, was divided into good power and bad power.

Skinner saw good and bad power as further divisible into human power and natural power. Helpfully, for the listener at least, bad

power was always human and good power was always natural. There was little room for confusion here.

Skinner had no doubt that bad/human power emanated from a series of institutions and people, many of whom he was forced to have contact with far too often for his own liking: there were the bastards who ran the dole office; there was the police; there were the courts; the government; multinational companies; arms dealers; the entire capitalist system; and, most recently, the national park gits who'd forced him to move his caravan, and the owner of The Dragon who'd had him barred after an altercation provoked entirely by the bad power that resided in Jack Bach and Will Garage.

Skinner was adamant that good/natural power was all around them, in the trees, in the rocks, in the rivers, and, of course, most powerfully in the lines. Fortunately, people still had access to this, although it seemed to be a mighty big advantage if you didn't have any money, or a job (which might bring you into a polluting proximity to the citadels of bad/human power), or a great deal of land — legally owning the trees, rocks and rivers was a surefire way of stanching the flow of their gifts.

Skinner believed that some places had more good/natural powers than others, and that some peoples, during certain epochs, had been more connected to it than others. Now it just so happened that Anglesey was more or less overflowing with good/natural power, and that at one time its druids, and their Celtic charges, had been some of its most dutiful and devoted worshippers. Not that this was the case now, far from it: the power remained, but, overall, the present day inhabitants were a sorry bunch of backsliders, an unrepentant, ignorant and ungrateful shadow of their forebears.

Now Gemma had to admit that this was not, by any stretch of the imagination, the sum total of Skinner's many reflections — on the contrary, he had a near endless supply of ideas and opinions — but that, if pressed, you could always trace them back to this set of fundamentals.

* * *

Looking out the caravan window one rather dank December afternoon, Gemma tried, as she had on several occasions, to imagine Skinner's invisible grid, the criss-crossed lines that apparently pulsed beneath the dirt. A close examination of the landscape revealed lines aplenty on the surface: hedgerows and stonewalls, barbed wire draped between posts, the borders between woodlands and fields, a narrow lane snaking its way down towards the sea. These lines were not orderly, not enigmatically straight and symmetrical — as the leys supposedly were — but neither were they absolutely random; generations of farmers, Gemma sensed, had carried and built and slashed and hammered them into place. They did not seem to be altogether permanent either: in some places you could see the remnants of forgotten walls, their stones strewn across the fields, stepped over by flocks of sheep and herds of cows oblivious to the long battles for liberation their ancestors must once have waged. Whatever pattern might lurk under the ground, she thought, it had little in common with that above. If one was elemental and eternal, the other was shifting and porous; if one lay miraculously fixed over centuries and millennia, the other reeked of old, forgotten sweat.

Turning from the window she reached out and picked up a cup, in which a powdery green and blue mould had begun to form over a teabag; two rollie butts lolled beside it, splaying shards of tobacco into a grey residue of leftover tea and tar.

"I'm gasping for a cuppa," Skinner croaked, emerging from behind the smokestained floral curtain that separated the mattress they slept on from the rest of the caravan. It was a dark, murky afternoon, and though it wasn't raining there was a heavy wetness in the atmosphere as though the raindrops had simply halted in mid-air and hung there, suspended in a grey, saturated lethargy. This gloomy dampness had seeped inside and Skinner shuffled into a clammy half-light, his black dreadlocks dangling like dead eels around his bony forehead. His clothes which, as usual, he'd slept in, clung to him like seaweed, a motley costume of patches and tassels and scarves, once colourful but now faded and washed out, making him look for all the world like some derelict, shipwrecked harlequin.

"I'm just making some," Gemma replied, throwing the contents of the cup out the window and pouring in the tea.

"You'll never guess what that wanker Giles is planning," Skinner barked over his cup, leaving a short dramatic pause to emphasise the enormity of the infamy he was about to unveil.

"Only a road, a road right fucking through the field here!"

"Why does he need to build a road here?" Gemma asked, trying to muster the requisite outrage at such evidence of the machinations of human power.

"To get to that frigging tower he's rebuilding, that's why. So he can bus in all his fatcat mates to sit around up there drinking gin and tonics, that's why. So the whole bunch of them can look around and see where to build their next holiday home or stable for their daughters' little pony or car park for their fucking landrovers."

Gemma pictured the muddy track that went from the lane across the field to the caravan and attempted to feel revulsion at the prospect of a new, gravel road going right past the front door.

"Well, what does Jack Cucu think about it?" she asked.

"Cucu'll think it's a great way to pocket some easy money, that's what he'll think. He couldn't give a shit about these fields as long as he gets some extra cash out of them. He's got no idea about their real value, about what they are, he's just a mercenary little shit and you know it, Gemma." Skinner's anger had begun to crackle and flame in the dampness, although Gemma still felt the need to light two bars on the gas heater in the corner. This was a habit Skinner had when talking, to act as though someone had foolishly contradicted him, even if they hadn't actually said anything. In fact Gemma did not know at all if Cucu was a mercenary shit. Jack was the farmer who let Skinner park his caravan on his field for fifteen pounds a week, which seemed quite generous on the face of it. When she first met him she'd been terribly curious about his name, thinking, when she first heard it, that he must be a little doolally. But he hadn't seemed in the least cucu when she spoke to him, just a rather nice old man who was tolerantly bemused by his new lodgers. Gemma had discovered afterwards in the village that his father had been the original Cucu. He'd never really got over his experiences during the war, people said, and one evening he'd been found naked in the small river that ran past The Dragon, clutching a shotgun and imploring passers-by not to disturb his patrol. Cucu had been passed down to his son as a patronymic, inherited along with his land and animals — maybe not the legacy one would have chosen, but one that Jack didn't seem unduly bothered about. Gemma could never work out why Skinner disliked him so much. To be sure, there was Jack's complicity with bad power, his dealings with CAP grants and government subsidies, but that hardly constituted collaboration on a Vichean scale; Jack's conspiring was on a pretty damn minor scale however you looked at it. No, Skinner's bile seemed based on some murkier element in the Skinner cosmology, some other infringement. For a while Gemma had struggled to put her finger on it, until one day.

They'd taken the bus into town to sign on and as they got off a couple of teenagers had sneered "Sais hippy" at Skinner. Now the hippy part he must have been familiar enough with, but the Sais bit sent him ranting and raving through the whole afternoon, stamping along the pavements amongst the old women on their way to the Post Office, thundering past poor, confused sightseers, waving his head around in a great fury like some new age Medusa. It was that little epithet, harmlessly descriptive on one level, but on another evocative of an unassailable exclusion, of an immemorial unbelonging, that roused Skinner's ire. Because, Gemma had come to realise, Skinner felt himself to be the custodian of the island's ancient legacy, its oldest, most potent, secrets, and for this one word to hint that it never had been, nor ever would be, his, was unbearable. Whatever forgotten and perverse migration had led his relatives to Hampshire, Skinner truly felt that he had a special access to this land and its power. In this scheme of things Giles was an easy adversary; but Cucu was different, was one of those, like the kids on the bus, who could sneer Sais at him, that could make him the interloper, the invader, the vandal, all the things he wanted everybody else to be.

"Well, I'll tell you this Gemma," Skinner snorted over his tea. "I'm not going to let them get away with this, I'm not."

"But what can you do?" she asked.

"I'll think of something," he said, "you'll see."

* * * *

Gemma spent the next morning in a thick, grey gloom of boredom. There was no TV in the caravan, no radio even, nothing. The previous day's static wetness had turned into a heavy droning rain that thumped oppressively onto the caravan's aluminium roof and ran off in monotonous streams into the field. This perpetual dripping and sloshing, unalleviated by other sounds, made her think of Chinese water torture, of how men were supposed to have been driven to madness by drops falling on their foreheads. She could see clearly how it worked: the sound magnified into a huge, reverberating drumming, obliterating all other sound until it came to claustrophobically inhabit the space around you, the soundwaves seeping into you until your pulse followed its percussive rhythm, your heart beating out its drip, drip, drip. Death by boredom, gradual, accretive; death's symphony, played out on a thousand little faucets, conducted by a metronome. Why was she here? She pictured her life in a series of bathetic film scenes: girl argues with parents; girl is unhappy with unjust world — parents and world synonymous; friends go to university, girl thinks it's a waste of time, that it's not real enough; girl meets other people who are unhappy with the world; girl ends up living in a leaky caravan in North Wales; the credits roll over a background of saturated green; drip, drip, drip. And the worst thing was that she couldn't really work out the impetus that had led her on, couldn't really remember why she had been so unsatisfied. Everything now felt like attenuation, a drift away from some forgotten passion into aimlessness, into motions she went through, not knowing why or what for or where they would, or could, take her. Somewhere there was the memory of idealism, or something like it, of a purpose and a desire, but that was sealed away now, sheltering from the dark, drizzly world.

Gemma picked up Skinner's favourite book, or she assumed it was his favourite, there being few others in the caravan. He was more a pamphlet kind of man, or its modern equivalent, the downloaded internet article. The book was called *The Celtic Wheel Of Life*, and had been written by Walter Copaut, who introduced himself as a Celtic medicine man. Flicking through the introduction, Gemma read

As you learn about the Celtic Wheel of Life you will learn about the nature of the universe and the power and teachings of the Celtic vision. You will learn about the cycles of death and life that govern our world and that we have so much forgotten.

Mr Copaut was very interested in forgotten things and, as Gemma read on, the introduction turned to his childhood

As a child, I was enthralled by Celtic myth and legend. More than anything else in the world I wanted to believe in magic. But, as I grew older, that magic seemed harder and harder to believe in. It has taken me many years to find it again and to sense how it is a real thing, something still powerful and that can still heal and help us. Most people think that there is no magic left in the world, but I sense it everyday, and have written this book to help others reconnect to it.

Looking out the window Gemma felt a little sceptical about the world's resources of magic. Cucu, cloaked in a tattered green oilskin coat, was hammering some barbed wire around a blackthorn tree at the bottom of the field and didn't look in the least like some latter day Merlin. Two sodden sheep were pressed up against a hedgerow and seemed unlikely interpreters of nature's wisdom. In fact it was simply too cold and wet to imagine any magic wanting to alight in this landscape; maybe it only lived in equatorial countries and spoke Spanish and drank sangria. Walter Copaut, however, remained nothing if not insistent

The Celtic world is a rich landscape of limitless possibilities where you can learn from everything, be it human, animal, plant or stone. If you close your mind to the possibility of other realms of existence, then you deny yourself the wisdom and understanding that can show you how to find happiness, health and fulfilment.

Now no-one, Gemma thought, was more desirous of other realms of existence than her, only her idea of those realms was far more modest than Walter's. Forget talking birds and singing stones and prancing fairies, she'd be happy, healthy and fulfilled right now with a proper toilet, some central heating and a television. In fact, Walter was beginning to piss her off. If this Celtic way of life was full of gentle magic and benign vision, an ancient antidote to modern misery, then why was Skinner such a splenetic, angry man? How had he converted Walter's bland but amiable world of soothing energies, restorative cycles and invisible wonders into a possessive paranoia, a nagging righteousness, a way of fighting the world? If Walter was the type of druid you got in comic books, who pottered around picking herbs and mistletoe and boiling up pleasantly intoxicating potions, then Skinner was the kind you found in Roman annals, sacrificing virgins in oak groves and burning children in wicker men. Maybe she was being a little unfair to Walter; it was Skinner who was pissing her off.

Gemma turned the gas heater up to four bars and watched as the flame spluttered up the white, honeycomb filaments, glowing blue at first before flecks of orange spread across and settled into fluttering rectangles. Try as you might you just couldn't get warm in this place. The heat from the gas was thick and faintly nauseous. As it permeated the front of the caravan the smell of damp and mould grew stronger, as though this treacly warmth were feeding a legion of hibernating spores that now stretched out and luxuriated in the air around her. Skinner had begun to rustle behind the floral curtain.

"I'm gasping for a cuppa," he croaked, stretching out his arms like a tattered parrot.

Gemma listened to the metallic patter of the rain on the roof. Walter had moved onto Celtic cosmology and was talking about spirals and circles, about the constancy of nature's cycles, of the comfort to be derived from being connected to The Great Wheel Of Being. As Gemma pictured that wheel it became slightly less comforting: the revolutions of the equinox became interminable repetitions; the rotations of the seasons became images of Sisyphean affliction. The wheel wasn't carrying her, it was crushing her.

"Get it yourself then, I'm busy!"

"Fuck, what's the bee in your bonnet?" replied Skinner. He paused for a moment, as though he might be waiting for an answer, and then began to energetically unravel a crumpled scroll of paper over the chipped, yellow plastic surface of the caravan's table, knocking over several cans of Spar lager in the process, from which oozed a black, yeasty sediment. Gemma watched in silence as he pored over the scroll. Its surface was a mixture of light green and brown, and was filled with undulating black lines that looped in uneven circular sweeps, some stretched far apart and some packed densely together. Set amongst these lines were others, some squares, some wavy oblongs, some thin rectangular strips. Skinner was holding a pen and a ruler in his hands, and had begun to draw yet another series of lines over the paper, thick, dark, straight lines that cut mercilessly through all the others.

"What's that then?" Gemma asked after watching him for several minutes.

"It's a map, what did you think it was."

"What are you doing with a map?"

"I'm marking the lines on it."

"What lines? It looks like it's got enough bloody lines on it already."

"I'm drawing on the ley lines, if you must fucking know. Those others are just contour lines and property lines; you know, to mark hills and stuff, and the boundaries of fields."

Gemma remembered when these had been Skinner's lines of seduction, how she had sat supine and high while they washed over her, unquestioning, attentive, letting them touch her like fingers. Today they were annoying her. She let her scepticism bristle.

"Well how do you know where the ley lines are, you told me they were invisible. If they're made up of energy how are you supposed to work out where exactly they are? Stick lightbulbs in the dirt!"

"There's lots of ways to follow them, if you know how. You can sense them with divining rods and things. And you can hear them too."

"How the hell can you hear them?"

"Christ, what is this, twenty questions? Look, it's a fact that the earth gives off its own music, right, it sings. All the old Celts knew it. And if you want proof there's experiments and all sorts been done. These two Japanese guys did these tests and found a weird humming noise coming from the ground and it was all these notes crammed together, and wherever they did these tests they found the same noise. Only most people can't hear it because it's loads of octaves below what the ear can normally pick up, but it's there and nobody can explain it. You can read about it if you want, I downloaded it ages ago."

"And you're saying you can hear it?"

"Yeh, I can. I get this vibrating sensation in my body when I'm close to the lines and then, if I concentrate, it becomes a humming sound, like a bee at first but then different, like a lullaby or something. And I can follow it, as long as I stay on the line."

"So you've been following these lines around like some rat after the pied piper?"

But Skinner had become too absorbed in drawing on the map to notice her now. The only sound in the caravan was the drumming of the rain, beating out the sky's monotonous melodies.

****

That afternoon Cucu came knocking on the door. Skinner had disappeared hours before and so Gemma invited him in for tea. He stood for a time on the metal doorstep, looking slightly embarrassed and tentative, as though expecting to enter some den of bewildering, modern iniquity. He turned his eyes down towards the ground as he spoke and his voice was a deep whisper: "I'm sorry to bother you luv, it's just I wanted a word with Skinner. Nothing serious like, I just wanted to ask about the stones at the bottom of the field." A thin steam drifted off his oilskin as he stood beside the heater, smelling of outdoors and animals, and he remained standing there, awkwardly, until Gemma pulled up a chair and invited him to take off his coat and sit down. Cucu wasn't used to being in other people's houses, or caravans for that matter. He sat on the chair but kept his coat on.

"It's not that I mind or anything, but I'll be moving silage there soon and they'll be in the way." Gemma noticed the carefulness with which he spoke, the way his diffidence extended to the words he used, as though they too were a slightly alien environment, one that he must enter gently, lest it surprise or betray him. She'd noticed this the first few weeks after arriving, how everyone spoke to her slowly, as though she might be slightly deaf, enunciating each line of speech delicately and purposely like a spider spinning a web over some unseen gulf of silence. She still noticed it now, everytime she trekked down to the Spar in the village, how the loud, quick murmuring within receded when she opened the door and went inside, how it slowed to a quiet, clipped succession of polite inquiries: "Gemma, how are you settling in"; "Yes, it's awful this weather isn't it"; "Of course, that's on Jack's land isn't it." And it wasn't just suspicion, it was more like everyone was withholding some hidden thing, a secret that they didn't even know they kept but had kept so long that the concealment of it was the only reminder that it existed.

Cucu sipped his tea like it had been poured into Sunday best china and not a chipped mug with Greenpeace scrawled on it.

Gemma asked him questions about the farm, about how long his family had owned it, what it had been like growing up here. She didn't quite know why she was asking him these questions, only that she suddenly felt terribly lonely and out of place and knew that Skinner would make these feelings worse, but that somehow Cucu, dripping in his coat and mumbling over his tea, made them a little better. At first he seemed rather astonished that anyone would ask him such things, as though the answers were simply public knowledge, and that asking for them was like an explorer inquiring after the significance and value of some moth-eaten mat that his native guide knew full well was just an old blanket. But after a while he became more comfortable and garrulous, a bit pleased that someone might be interested in the stories that everybody else he spoke to already knew.

He told her how when he was a boy an old woman had lived in a stone cottage down in the fields beside the sea; that she'd had bright red hair and sometimes spoke in a strange language and that all the local kids thought she was a witch. Sometimes they'd snuck into her garden to steal apples and seen horrible dolls hanging from the rafters like dead children. He told her how his father had seen a ghost in their yard, a tall, ugly man, all dressed in yellow, who glowed in the dark. He told her about the times when he was a boy and they had made hay in this very field, cutting it with scythes and loading it with pitchforks, and how his nain had brought them all homemade barley water and lemonade to drink. He told her that Giles's tower had once been a working windmill, but that everyone thought it was an unlucky place because one of its owners, many years back, had hung himself in it. The girl who worked for the family had found him inside, dangling on a rope, with the sails still wheeling around outside. Nobody'd known why he did it. Cucu said a Polish man had once lived in the cottage beside the track down to the sea. He'd arrived during the war and when they were boys he'd always stop him and his friends and give them currant buns. After a while all the steam had evaporated from Jack's coat and the air seemed warm and comfortable. Gemma got up to make more tea but Jack looked up and said he really must get going, that he was sorry to bother her about the rocks and it wouldn't be any trouble really but he had to put that silage down soon. Gemma said not to worry, she'd sort things out. And then he went out the door and she watched him shuffle into the rain, his tattered oilskin flapping slightly in the wind.

After he left Gemma looked out at the tower, its pale stone standing out against the grey sky, and thought about the poor man who had died there. She wondered what had happened to him? What had made him do it? Maybe all these sad, wet days had simply taken their toll, that the rain had beaten once too often on his roof, and he had followed this melancholy drumming into despair. Water torture. Listening to Jack she had thought how every story was really an elegy, how they were populated with dead people, and took place in ruined houses, and happened in dead times. Outside, the landscape was just a huge, patterned graveyard, each field a plot, each wall a gravestone, each cluster of trees a forgotten bouquet of flowers. She had thought about Skinner's map, and how maps were just a story about the ground beneath, an epitaph written in cold, mute lines. Jack had only asked her one question, her own question repeated: why was she here. And she knew she didn't have an answer and she knew she didn't want to keep on not having one. And more than anything else she wanted to go home.

* * * *

The next morning Skinner headed off, map in hand, down the field towards his stones. Gemma had asked him about them the night before and he'd got terribly cryptic, and she'd become terribly annoyed. "What do you need with a bunch of old rocks?" she'd said. "It's none of your business," he'd replied tersely. "I don't understand what it is you've got to be so fucking secretive about. I mean what can you do with a load of stones that needs to be kept so mysterious."

"Look," Skinner spat out. "I'm marking them out and it needs to be done properly. I'm not having that wanker building a road over them without a fight so I'm marking them. And you can't just throw them down, there's chants and prayers and things you need to say when you're doing it."

"Christ, it's not those lines again. What the hell difference is it going to make, you dumping rocks on Cucu's field. He's got to use them you know and he's doing us both a favour letting us stay here."

"Like fuck is he doing us a favour!" shouted Skinner. "He's making fucking money out of us is what he's doing. And you can't see that. I mean when did you become so sodding useless anyway, you're no better than the rest of them!"

"And what's the use in what you're doing?" Gemma asked.

"Tell me what exactly you hope to achieve doing whatever you're planning to do?"

"You'll see," he said.

It had been like an awful parody of a playful lover's tiff: the withheld secret, the relentless importuning, the winking, teasing evasion. Only there was very little love involved and the evening had ended with Skinner screaming at her for letting Cucu inside the caravan. Finally he'd lurched towards her, catching her with a punch that left her crumpled in the corner. Afterwards, sitting alone beside the heater's sickly heat, Gemma had looked out the window at a few bedraggled stars that had emerged between the clouds. Skinner's hand still felt huge on her forehead, while inside her stomach felt small and shrunken. Her arms and legs dangled around her as though they had lost all strength and volition, like she was a discarded puppet. She had sat there astonished at the capacity for one blow to empty someone of all will, all outrage, all anger, to leave them temporarily so vacant, caught in this amazed, starlit stillness. And into that stillness came the thought that all the powers in the world, whether they bubbled under the earth or were written into charters and laws, whether they worked through magic or machination, in the end came down to only this.

Watching Skinner stride down across the field this morning — so different from Cucu who walked diffidently across even his own land — Gemma thought how difficult it was for people to protect themselves from other people's anger, from other people's ideas and beliefs, that the closer you were the more they pushed them upon you, and nothing, no ironic detachment, no sceptical accommodation, would placate them. People were not bound in circles and spirals and cycles, they were meshed together across tensile lines, barbedwire boundaries and borders that you could reach briefly and gently through or else smash with your fist. And whichever option you chose they would not go away and you would not stop trying to breach them and you would not stop trying to protect them.

She followed him outside. He was standing on the winter grass, a thin covering of green that spilt cold mud onto his boots. The night's chilly clarity had dispersed; wet wreathes of drizzle had drifted over everything. The hushed swirling wetness was like wool, it swaddled the noise of the morning. A crow flew above them, its hoarse cry struggling through the air. Somewhere a cow was lowing. He was standing on the winter grass with a stone in his hand, he was making a line of stones, placing one after the other until they began to stretch across the field. It was like the whole morning had turned into slow motion: each stone after the other, stretching across the field. She could hear his voice but she could not hear the words. His voice was like praying, low and whispered and liturgical. But she could not hear the words, only the cadence which was like rain. The side of her face was hurting. She wanted to ask him what he was doing but she didn't want to ask him anything. The crow swooped but you couldn't hear its wings. There were tiny spiderwebs spun between the thin grass, they were so delicate she feared the rain would break them. His stone lines cut across the field, heaped upon the crushed grass. She began to walk towards the lane. As she got further away the only thing she could hear was her own breathing, which would damage nothing.

The Tower

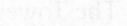

A tower in the centre, blurs of green on either side funnelling towards it, swirling, eddying, vertiginous. This was the view from his glass porch, a week old and still smelling of fresh pine and window putty. The horizon he had built for himself, to enjoy on spring mornings and long summer evenings, to invite his friends to admire and envy. A tower set in a blur of verdure. A vertigo horizon. An emerald whirlpool. The injustice of it rankled, burning and aching: to have made this place, to have put everything in order for a view that his own eyes would not deliver to him. Christ, he had done everything, surpassed every expectation, and yet this thing had kept apace with all his triumphs, feeding off them, augmenting itself with every success he built as a bulwark against it. Because he knew now that what lurked behind his eyelids was no inscrutable medical process — his doctors talked about it like some fucking divine mystery — but a thing, a wriggling, active, malicious thing. The snake in his garden. And he felt now that his whole life, since the day it had wormed unnoticed into his sockets, had been no more than one long effort to build a cage that might hold it.

* * * *

"Derrick, Jack Bach just called. He said the wood for the tower steps wouldn't be here until Monday." The voice of Cathy Giles, his wife. Née Cathy Geraghty, his lover, twenty something years ago. The years before it arrived. Cathy and Robert fucking la-de-da Buckley riding on the Wirral sands — posh wanker and Irish girl holding hands on the dunes, him seething and jealous and helpless. There was nothing he could do about it. He'd worked for Cathy's old man, who'd owned a cowboy building outfit called Geraghty Construction: jobs done quick, cheap materials, cheap labour; mick relatives everywhere, crawling out of the woodwork to do dodgy plumbing, electrics, the works. Robert was from the Wirral upper-crust, his father a barrister in Liverpool who had moved his family to the rural purlieus of the city, a countryside suburbia where his offspring could live out a gentrified daydream away from the banks of the filthy Mersey. It was the horses that got Derrick: four of them molly-coddled in a local stable, with Robert striding around in a pair of flouncy jodhpurs lord-of-the-manor style. It was where he met Cathy, whose old man had bought his pride and joy a pony, half to indulge her, half to display his own burgeoning wealth. Successful cowboys needed horses.

On his free Sundays Derrick had followed them, the rusty clinking of his bicycle shadowing the clip-clopping of horseshoes, an indigent echo caught up amongst the background hum of unseen insects. Following them down through winding lanes thick with honeysuckle, hot and sweet, curling its languorous scent around him. Following them until they broke out into the open sweep of undulating dunes and tufted hillocks that smoothed the land into the sea; a wide, borderless horizon where sand and water met in one long, indistinct caress. And as they moved into that distance he had followed them with his eyes, spreading his vision across the pale, washed out interface of sand and sea and sky, magnifying it, moving through it, until he sensed it dissolve into an inchoate swirl of elements, primordial, preterite, where all things had not yet been made, where possibility darted in sea-gull swoops and crawled half-formed towards the shore. All things possible: Cathy beneath him, adoring, submissive, flashing thighs like Leda, opening them; his tightening fingers a fleshy nowhere, an adjunct to the crimson slipperiness stained on his retina, oozing behind closed lids. All things. The sudden jerk and the second more softly, splattering his sperm on the sand. And then the sad after-lull, whose vacancy began to fill with delicious images of dominion: Robert his minion, Cathy his wife, herds of horses — his own.

"Christ! when did he call?" Derrick called back, trying to mask the exasperation that he always feared would betray him, make him once more the building site foreman browbeating some tardy supplier.

"Is it that important dear?" asked Cathy in a lazy, preoccupied voice. Derrick breathed deeply and inhaled almost a quarter century of accumulated irritation. His little Irish princess, though now grown fat off his land, who never worried about the details, about how things got done, about what was or wasn't important. Spoiled by her father, and then spoiled by him. Because having her was the important thing, even now when she had become plain and portly, the actuality of who and what she was less essential to him than her role in vindicating all that he had made of himself. Owning one's fantasies had simply become one more of life's ample burdens. The sand had drifted over his desire twenty years ago.

"It's fine dear, I'll deal with it." Yes, he would deal with it, concealing his annoyance behind the bluff largesse he had put on ever since buying Plas Gwalia. It was how he had always dealt with these people, always impeccably generous, always open-handed and willing to overlook the liberties they took with him, their inefficiencies and slapdash arrangements. He made allowances for the odd bale of straw that didn't arrive, the feed delivery promised for Tuesday that arrived on Saturday; for the man who promised to mend his dry stone wall in a couple of days and dawdled on it for a couple of weeks; for the stray sheep or bullock that broke into his garden and trampled his wife's petunias. He let it all slide and more, paying them over the odds, lending out his new machinery, employing locals when outside workers would have done the job quicker and better. Of course, he could have taken advantage of them. If he was to be honest about it, most of his neighbours weren't exactly the brightest bulbs in the bunch; good, simple people but just hicks really. And when he thought of the more unscrupulous characters he had worked with in Merseyside — Jack Geraghty and his fly-by-night crew sprung to mind — he had to admit how bloody straight up he'd treated them. Even the land he'd bought here — twenty acres surrounding his house — had been paid for at a rate at least double what it was actually worth. He'd given a ludicrously ample amount of cash for fields used for little more than grazing and the odd paltry crop of silage, never once making the local farmers feel like he was doing them a favour (which undoubtedly he was), but letting them think that he was simply paying a fair price. Always accommodating, always lavish, because he was not here to make money (he'd made enough for one lifetime, probably more) but to make solid the world he had glimpsed in an evanescent juncture of sea and sky and land.

And why this place, he sometimes thought, why choose here when it could have been anywhere? It had been the first summer after their marriage, the marriage which had been the initial realisation of what he'd mapped out while hunkered down in the sand dunes. Because not a man to renege, even upon his daydreams, Derrick had worked furiously towards them: saving his money, becoming Jack's right hand man, buying his own properties and refurbishing them, waiting for Robert to attenuate and vanish while he accumulated and solidified, while he got rich in a way Robert and his father, and even Jack, never would. And sure enough Robert had ponced off to university to entertain his new la-de-da mates with his tales of the talent at home, and Geraghty, his bog Irish dreams of social mobility shattered, had pushed his daughter towards the next best thing, the thing he really understood — real money.

That summer they had travelled down to Rhyl with the legions of Scousers that even then Derrick was eager to dissociate himself from, and which Rhyl itself seemed to embody. Neon signs set over tawdry pavements, littered by greasy chip papers; Ferris wheels careering over decrepit fairgrounds, their sickly revolutions lit up by flashing lights made somehow wan in the salt-sad evening darkness, looking down on asphalt caked with mushed hot-dogs and congealing onions, strewn with putrid, pinky candy floss, toffeed apples with rotted cores. The serried ranks of caravans stretched, like some colony of aluminium chrysalises, down to the ancient sea — birthing butterflies of plastic detritus that were uplifted in the breeze and sent swirling over the waters. Rhyl, the Scouse subjunctive, what filled the January dreams on the docks, was part of what Derrick felt he must unlearn and repudiate. Wandering through the fish-and-chip streets with Cathy that summer, Derrick, a professional and experienced refurbisher, transmuted what in his teens had been a landscape of promise and pleasure into vistas of tackiness and cheapness. Derrick's business had taught him that class meant something that looked older, something a bit more antique: original oak beams, traditional fireplaces, old stones. The next summer he took his wife further west, towards the castled coasts of Gwynedd and Anglesey; ten years later he owned a piece of them.

****

Old stones! A heap of them on a hill. The blur of mountains in the east, blue sea-shadows spreading to the north and west, a rolling patchwork of green oozing south.

"A commanding view, I'm sure you'll agree Mr Giles," proclaimed the estate agent from Bangor. "Of course this comes with the property," he said, spreading his hand over the crumbling tower. "It used to be a working windmill but, as you can see, it's been abandoned for some years now."

Derrick looked out over the view that for fifty thousand pounds was his to command. Down to his left was the cottage where he'd live, small for now, with two windows looking out at him like cat eyes, furtive and wary, watching. He'd get rid of them. Looking closer he saw crumbling whitewash, a roof of slates with gaps here and there, door frames rotted down to a plaquey, carious brown; his eyes moving with forensic care and his breath held in gently like a dentist's. It needed work, a lot of work, but it had potential, yes it certainly had potential. Further to the left an old Massey Ferguson wheezed its way through dry, rutted fields towards rickety sheds of rusty corrugated iron and weathered concrete. This was the neighbouring farm which, if he was honest, Derrick thought to be bloody unsightly; with its accumulations of twisted and obscure metal that he imagined could only be the relics of moribund machinery (though every now and then the farmer would hitch one of them to the Massey and vanish on some mysterious errand); its pebble-dashed bungalow; its scowling pack of mangy, yellow-eyed sheepdogs that lurked in yards and hedgerows, breeding flies and dropping ticks; its treacherous labyrinths of barbed wire hidden like vicious slug trails in the hedges. Unsightly, no doubt about it, and inconvenient too, but okay for now, thought Derrick, imagining how he would tell city friends that what he liked about the property was its authentic rural surroundings:

"Yes," he would tell them, "I like to be in a part of the country that's worked, you know, not some glorified golf course or something." Besides, Derrick thought, the farmer looked about as old and clapped out as his farm. There would be an opportunity to expand soon enough. Those sheds could be made into stables with a bit of work.

Standing there on the hill he could see it all so clearly: the tangled blackthorn hedges and walls of stony rubble transmogrified into tidy fields enclosed by regular pine fences; the manky sheep replaced by horses; and, in the middle of it all, the tower, restored and imposing, looking down on all of the land around. A commanding view, it was most certainly a commanding view. Standing there on his hill, Derrick remembered an old painting in a gallery Cathy had dragged him to. In it a man stood on an elevated rise, wrapped in elegant silks with two spaniels at his feet and an ebony cane in his hand, while below him spread an orderly succession of fields, dotted symmetrically with oaks and copses of willow; the whole scene bathed in neo-classical stillness, each detail clear and exquisite, every object pristine and proportioned and harmonious. A man surrounded by his land. Larks hovered in pure azure, frozen into the sky; a pheasant stood in the middle distance, each feather distinct and refulgent in the static sunbeams; the hills in the far background etched on a horizon bordered securely by a golden frame.

"I don't think you'll find a more panoramic spot on the whole island, Mr Giles," said the estate agent, spreading out his arms. Derrick followed them with his eyes and oozing green displaced the gold, blue shadows smudged the horizon, the larks took flight into sickly, strobic blurs of black. It was as though his eyes had become the palette of some demented water-colourist. Not here, he thought, not here too.

****

"A rare condition, Mr Giles," twanged the doctor a bit smugly, "an extremely rare condition. I get ten, maybe twenty, cases of this a year."

"Cases of what?" Derrick asked, slightly exasperated. He was paying a lot of money to be patronised by this Yank opha-whateverthefuckitwas-ologist.

"You've got to see someone," Cathy had said. "I can't put up with your little tantrums every time you go out to look at some field." Doctors and opticians had given him referral after referral, sticking his head in various outlandish contraptions, shining blue lights and orange lights and red lights into his eyes, pouring phosphorescent dyes into them, asking him to look at circles and lines and all sorts of crap. He hated them looking into his eyes, somehow worried at what they might see in his sockets. Not the evidence of a disease necessarily, but the trace of things he had already seen, fearing that they might possess the power to reconstruct images out of some optic residue sedimented beneath his lids, excavating his eyeballs as though they were archaeologists of vision and memory. Sitting there, the light peering in at him, he became fiercely proprietorial, inwardly guarding the restored tower, the frozen larks, Cathy silhouetted against the juncture of land and sky, a stain on the sand.

"Retinitis pigmentosa, Mr Giles. It's a name we give to a group of diseases that affect the retina." Outside, on the grassy forecourt of the hospital, someone started up a lawnmower and the noise flickered gently against the windowpane like a tongue. The doctor shifted his weight in his leather chair, making a faint hissing sound. Afterwards it was that sound that Derrick remembered most clearly, not the name of his disease, but that sibilant expulsion of air. On the phone to Cathy he'd struggled to remember details from the doctor's diagnosis: photoreceptor cells, rods and cones, macula. He'd tried to recall the picture he'd had shown to him, but could only think of a circle with a triangle inside it.

"It degenerates these rods and cones things inside the eye... no, they're not really rods and cones they're cells... Christ! I don't know what kind of cells... no, it's not fucking contagious." The air whooshing out, squeezing its way through invisible holes in the leather: his eyeball a balloon, leaking vision like helium. And no way to stop it. Twenty years, the doctor had said, twenty years it'd been eating holes in his eye; half his life bleeding sight. And when it had finished? When it was emptied, what then? When he went to bed that night he was afraid to switch off the light.

****

"I don't care if the lazy bastards have to work all night," Derrick shouted across the yard, "but they're going to make up the time they've lost today." It was so hard to maintain a pose of equanimity when he had to deal with these work-shy buggers. Time meant nothing to them.

"We'll 'ave it done by Tuesday, Derrick, don't you worry

mate." And what was Tuesday, Tuesday was next Friday, just like Thursday was usually next Saturday. Days running into weeks, weeks running into months: time seeping away. He'd see them, punctual as you like, rolling into The George on Fridays and Saturdays and every other day of the week as far as he could tell, but come Monday they'd arrive in dribs and drabs with hollow eyes and ashen faces and aching bodies. Of course, he'd been young once himself, but he'd never been so cavalier with his work. He'd known what he'd wanted, knew what he needed to do and where he was going. It was their lack of ambition that irritated Derrick, the way they lived their lives as though life were simply some slapdash arrangement, something you got handed and then just made do with, fiddling with the edges now and then but never changing the bold outline. It was like they could never see beyond the day they lived in, bounded clearly on one side by The George and on the other, less bloody clearly, by their work at his place. There was no plan, no bigger picture. Why else did they never leave? Living out their time in the pebble-dashed council houses their parents had lived in before them, hitched to the first slut they'd managed to get up the duff, drifting from casual job to casual job. Time seeping and them just seeping along with it, catching hold of any flotsam that happened to coast by. He'd chosen to come here, made something of himself and picked where he wanted to own. Proactive! Derrick liked the word and used it often enough in his livingroom sermons in front of the select congregation of well-to-do locals who he occasionally assembled in his place. "You've got to be proactive," he would say, unveiling the foundations of his success. "See what needs to be done and get in there and do it," Derrick would intone, taking his life as exemplary text and his trips to America (business he let everyone think, not some oph-whatever-gist) as divine ordinance. "They know how to do business there," he'd tell them. "It doesn't matter where you're from or what you do, they see an opportunity and go for it." Proactive! Derrick pictured himself staring clear-eyed into an inchoate future, navigating paths and possibilities, charting his destinations, an intrepid mariner looking backwards at the deadbeats bobbing aimlessly in his wake.

"All night," he repeated, as though the impatient menace in his voice would conjure his errant workmen into place and have them toiling away with feudal obedience.

"Christ! What's the bee in your bonnet?" Cathy shouted back across the yard. "If they're not here then they're not here and making a song and dance about it won't change anything. Besides, I don't see what the bloody rush is — it's not like we need the thing to live in or anything."

Derrick wanted to shout back to her that that wasn't the point, that that wasn't the point at all; wanted to explain that he'd planned to finish it in a certain amount of time and these delays were affecting his plans; explain that it was getting the thing built that mattered. But it was hopeless trying to explain things to her, hopeless. If anything, she had more in common with his builders than him. He'd watch her bringing tea and cakes to Jack Bach and Bobby Tŷ Groes and Dewi Tew (they all had these stupid nicknames and he made a conscious point of not using them, though she did), and think how easily she got on with them, gossiping and laughing and flirting, flouncing around in her jodhpurs as they lounged away the afternoon on his time. Yes, more like them than him, which irked him because he had made this place for her, because she was supposed to be a part of it, not fade away into the surroundings. Maybe he hadn't worked hard enough on her, hadn't paid enough attention to shaping her as he had to his house? Looking at his property he felt a familiar surge of pride and gratification. Where once there had been two small rooms and a little upstairs loft, there was now a spacious livingroom and kitchen, flanked by the new guestrooms he had added to the original building, stretching it outwards until it resembled the broad facades of the ranch buildings he'd seen in his wife's horse magazines. Its squinty, cat eyes had vanished and been replaced by the new glass porch. The front lawn which, when they'd first arrived, had been a tangle of brambles, wild rose bushes, and gnarled apple trees, was now a tidy expanse of neatly cropped grass split in half by a path of polished, whorled stone, with white picnic tables nestled under cherry trees that exploded each spring with gaudy, pink blossoms and which each winter were draped in fairy lights that Derrick had bought to cheer up the murky darkness. Around the back he had pulled down the dilapidated stone walls and put in a wide gravel drive circled by sturdy pine fences, its entrance marked by two new marble pillars with Plas inscribed tastefully in gothic script on one and Gwalia on the other. It was indistinguishable from the poky little cottage it had been, Derrick thought, feeling the delicious pleasure of possession and assured in his sense that only metamorphosis was the true index of possession, that things only truly belonged to you when you had changed them, forced your imprint upon them, when you could look and see what you had willed and done. Derrick walked across his yard happily immune now to Cathy's short-sightedness, kicking at the occasional bramble that pushed stubbornly and defiantly through the gravel.

* * * *

They started arriving around twelve in the afternoon. Cathy and Derrick met them at the marble pillars, ushering their landrovers and BMWs into the yard where the two young spaniels Derrick had bought began yelping and careering around in hyperactive circles — try as he might he couldn't get the bastards to stand at heel. Up above, huge banks of cloud scuttled across the sky in a dizzy, kinetic procession that threw rapid bursts of light and shadow onto the land like some crazed photographer gone berserk with his flashbulbs. The guests made smalltalk as Derrick hurried them towards the diningroom, angrily aware that two fields away to his right the old farmer's bull had burst through a hedge to get to a herd of young heifers, where he was now happily sniffing their behinds amidst a deafening chorus of lowing and groaning and bellowing. Today of all days he thought, while discussing the weather with Mrs Evans, the local councillor's wife, trying to turn her attention towards the brass weather vane he'd installed on his chimney, which spun around to the east as the bull hoisted himself merrily onto a heifer's back. Today of all days! Everything had been so well planned. They were to have lunch in the new glass porch that looked out onto the hill where his restored tower stood;

then, afterwards, they would all drive up the road he had built and have cocktails on the tower roof, which he had made into a platform with stone ramparts. He'd imagined the whole day, the eating and the admiration, the drive up the hill, the climb up the spiral stairway and onto the tower's summit, the panorama spreading around them and melting into the perfect blue horizon. Derrick, with Cathy beside him — somehow a lot younger and prettier in his imagination — offering his view to his guests and receiving their appreciation. "This is quite some place," they'd say. Derrick's place, Derrick's tower, a heap of stones he'd made into a monument.

"That's quite a job you've done with the old windmill," said Councillor Evans, looking out the window over his quiche, "yes, quite some job!" Everyone's attention began to shift towards the window. Murmurs of congratulation broke out over plates of hors d'oeuvres, filtering their way to Derrick through crumbs of pastry and shrimp, echoing between glasses of Rosé and Chardonnay, until they swept around him in a gentle, clamorous tide, which, momentarily, he let carry him away. And then they started pointing! "Look at those ramparts," he heard someone say, thrusting a finger towards the hill. "Those are beautiful windows, Derrick, did you have them made especially," and again a finger, lunging cruelly into a distance where he couldn't follow. And then a whole phalanx of them, sharp and bristling like porcupine quills, prodding at the horizon, questions and comments raining down on him like broken glass. Outside the glass a smudge of green swirled in front of him, gathering blotches of tributary colour — tints of yellow and blue and brown — and accelerating upwards into a sickly, iridescent vortex that spiralled towards the slate-grey silhouette of the tower. Spiralling away, Derrick thought, sensing the horrible inversion whereby his vision flowed outwards, an irreversible, ineluctable momentum over which he had no control, no volition, taking everything from him. And the tower in the middle of it all, diminishing him, sapping him, drawing all he had into its cold, blind stones.

He heard Cathy outside, giving directions and making apologies for him, heard the crunch of tyres on the gravel and the dwindling sound of engines. Silence poured into the empty room, filling it momentarily before new sounds began to intrude. The thin droning of a tractor's engine riffled through the quiet, the dull hum of unseen insects expanded and receded outside the window, brushing the glass in brief crescendos before ebbing back into the hushed afternoon, and above them all the bull's frantic lowing, thick with desire, but somehow lonely and plaintive too, not quite the sound of desire but of desire's elegy, the sound of a longing almost forgotten, lost and irreclaimable, that foundered through the air before dispersing back into silence. The silver knife felt cool and smooth in his hand, almost gentle. He ran the edges over his fingers. Of course there would be pain, but if he got the leverage right, if he wedged it against the socket and pressed downwards, it should only be temporary. It was important that he stayed conscious, that he get both. And why should anyone be shocked, he thought, why was it so different from drawing rotten teeth. They served no purpose now. Was he supposed to just wait while it did this, while it took what was left, to sit helpless while it worked on him. The silver so smooth in his hand — it was in his hands, he could get rid of it now once and for all. Derrick imagined sitting in a darkness that he had made, and that would be forever his own.

The Importance of
Being Elsewhere

Jack Bach hadn't been small since he was fourteen years old. But names tend to stick, and usually you don't get to choose them, and once you do get saddled with one, well, as often as not, that's that. So here he was, twenty-five, almost six feet tall and built like a bullock, but in the world of local appellation his physical transformation counted for nothing — he might as well not have grown at all. Sometimes it annoyed him: to think that the distance between himself now and a decade before had been obliterated like this, that somehow, on some level, despite everything that had altered, he was still the little boy who had hated being little. Once you got squeezed into a name, however badly it turned out to fit, however constricting it came to be, there seemed no way out of it. Getting away from yourself was a great deal more difficult then he had ever imagined.

To his friends he was just Bachie.

Bachie was out picking magic mushrooms in the fields behind his house. From where he was standing, stooped over a watery cowpat (the bastards liked growing beside shit, which could make picking them pretty disgusting), he could just see the upstairs windows of his house. They were covered by an opaque sheen of condensation — the breath of his girlfriend and kid who were still sleeping — that looked pearly white in the morning light. He liked being up before them. To be honest, he felt claustrophobic when he woke up in the same room and sensed the air thick with their breath. Even though he'd had a year to get used to it there remained an element of surprise about the whole thing, as though this family had materialised while he was sleeping, or he had inadvertently woken up in someone else's life. If he lay there too long a slight panic would creep over him. How did this happen? What was he doing here? How could he reverse time back to that fateful night in the back of Bobby Tŷ Groes's transit van? But once he was up and out things felt more distant and spacious and uncluttered. Besides, these autumn mornings were often quite beautiful. There were two kinds really. There were the still, clear ones, when the sky was a thin, watercolour blue and the orange leaves of the oaks and sycamores hung quietly above you, when a hushed shiver of mist dawdled on the grass and the hedgerows were dotted with blood-red rosehips and plump blackberries. Then there were the wild, tumultuous ones, when the wind careered in from the west, salted with sea-spray from the straights, and threw everything into such a swirling confusion that sometimes it was hard to get your bearings even in familiar places.

This morning, thankfully, was of the former variety. Bachie looked up from the cowpat he was scrutinising and took a breath of the fresh, still air. The field he was standing in was long and wide, with several tall oak trees marooned like islands in the middle of it. Up to his right, in the distance, he could see the carious ramparts of the castle, rotted like old grey teeth, with two limp flags — a dragon and a Celtic cross — sleeping on its highest turrets. To his left, much closer, were the corrugated iron walls of the old factory, criss-crossed with broad seams of rust that looked like sedimentary deposits in ancient rock, its green paint peeling rapidly away as though in sympathetic homage to the autumnal surroundings. Out in front of him the main road made its way along the edge of a seawall, behind which the straights dozed placidly on a bed of mud and black, seaweed-strewn rocks. On the other side of the water an undulating line of mountains stretched out towards the Irish sea, its strangely human curves and contours giving the impression that some pot-bellied Gulliver had lain down and snoozed on the horizon. Through the soporific morning mist that still clung to the ground, Bachie could make out the lumbering shapes of old men and dogs, their outlines merging oddly in the hazy light and moving across the field like ponderous, mythological apparitions. During the rest of the year these would normally be the sole companions of his dawn excursions, but this peculiar autumn harvest brought out a whole new, and unlikely, legion of early-risers.

To the unknowing eye, these October mornings would have presented a heartening and healthy spectacle: the island's youth out rambling through the fields at the break of day like so many rosy-cheeked devotees of nature. There they would be — beneath the pink-fingered clasp of Dawn, wrapped in parkas, their heads ensconced in hooded tops, their jeans flaring onto the dewy grass — a piece of modern pastoral in search of an urn. The truth, of course, was that these morning revellers were in search of a very specific tincture in the spectrum of nature's wonders.

Magic mushrooms: nature's freebies. Ever since he'd first taken them, Bachie had been both surprised and amused that drugs should just grow wild like this, an autumnal boon available to anybody who knew what to look for, that nobody could stop you gathering. You could pick them on the police station forecourt and the only thing they could do you for was trespass. It was the one time of the year, just before the world began to contract into the wet and attritional winter darkness, when the landscape here seemed truly beneficent and open-handed. It reminded him of hunting for Easter eggs as a child; the anticipation and excitement, the feeling that every otherwise quotidian nook and cranny was the magical repository of some confectionery benediction; the way your humdrum surroundings became somehow charged and protean, could be changed any minute into chocolate. Not that these mushrooms looked quite so enticing. They were long-stemmed and spindly, with elongated conical caps. The heads of the caps were covered in an inky smudge but all the rest of the fungus was a limp, palsied white, the colour of those slugs and salamanders and things that live underground in caves and never see the light. They hardly looked like living things at all. Growing beside shit and rotting leaves they seemed to live off death and decay, to imbibe and metabolise it, transforming it into their own damp and flaccid bodies. And yet somehow, through this eerie alchemy was distilled their magic.

As he bent down once more to search the ground, Bachie caught sight of Bobby and Dewi Tew (quite portly, always had been) ambling towards him. Bobby was short and wiry, with thick black hair that this morning had risen up into a profusion of tangled cowlicks. Dewi's hair lacked such rebellious density and was plastered down on each side of a brutally straight centre parting; patches of pink flesh were visible between each thin and oily frond. Although he had a wide and jowly face, Dewi had a small and delicate mouth, out of which poured an unfeasibly substantial lungful of cigarette smoke, that hung for a moment in the air before drifting down to join the remnants of mist that clung to the grass.

"A-rright Bachie," he called out, his voice sounding huge in the quiet morning.

"A-rright," Bachie replied.

"Fokk, yer up early mate," Bobby croaked, unsettling a layer of obstinate, tarry mucus that clung to the inside of his throat.

"How many've you got?" Dewi asked.

"I dunno, thirty, forty maybe," Bachie replied.

"Well, that's a start then."

Bachie opened up a plastic Spar bag and the other two peered thoughtfully inside. After a few seconds Bobby said, "Yeah, forty I reckon." But the contents of the bag — twisted stems and flattened caps, mixed in with bits of grass and fragments of twigs and leaves — appeared, to Bachie anyway, far too jumbled and obscure for such exact calculations.

****

The kitchen felt intolerably hot and small after being outside all morning. There didn't seem to be enough space or air for all of them. Dewi was pushing aside a plate of congealed baked beans, crusted and dark orange on the surface, to make space on the table for his mug of white, sweet tea — four sugars. Bobby was spreading out the morning's pickings on a sheet of newspaper; underneath the stringy stems a bold headline declaimed "Bull Goes Berserk". Bachie didn't feel all that comfortable having them doing this here in his house. He could sense his girlfriend's smell, recent and warm, on everything. There was his kid's smell too, a cloying mixture of milk and vomit. It didn't seem right, bringing them in here.

"Where's yer missus?" Dewi asked.

"She's at her mother's place, with the kid."

"When's she back?"

"Couple of hours, I dunno really."

"Well, we can drop 'em 'ere then. Watch telly for a bit while we come up."

Bachie imagined his girlfriend walking into the house with his daughter and finding the three of them jabbering like idiots in front of the television. The room seemed to contract still further — the whole house felt like it was shrinking. He couldn't risk it happening.

"Nah, I don't fancy staying round 'ere. The George'll be open now — lets just neck 'em and go."

"Sounds a'right to me," said Dewi, shifting around on a wooden chair over the edges of which his broad buttocks overflowed.

Bobby was lifting up fingerfuls of shrooms and putting them in a silver kettle. They were still slippery and wet and appeared grey and lifeless, like something dredged up from the bottom of a pond; their darkened caps pointed out like dead black nipples. They didn't look like they should be here in his kitchen, which had a floor of bright, sickly, orange linoleum and a pattern of putrid pink roses on the walls. His kitchen was the colour of cartoons. The colour of heat and headaches too. It had been his grandmother's once, before she went loopy and started thinking that he was his grandfather and that she was sixteen years old; it was where she grew vegetables and waited for her already dead sons to come home from school, smiling in anticipation, surrounded by carrots and potatoes; before they took her to the home. This kitchen had felt warm and inviting once — when he was a boy — somewhere to eat sweets on the way home from school, but over the years it had come to seem livid and nauseous, as though her madness had somehow leaked out into the room.

The kettle began to boil. Bobby picked it up and started to pour the contents through a sieve into a big, chipped tea mug. The air began to smell like dirt, not healthy outdoor dirt, but old dirt, the kind you find on the floors of abandoned sheds, mildewed and fungoid.

"Who's first then?" Bobby asked, raising up the cup with a druidical flourish.

This was always the tricky bit. How many should you take? How many were there likely to be in the cup? Bachie began to calculate nervously. Altogether he reckoned they'd picked about two hundred, though he couldn't be sure about that — say two hundred and fifty, just to be on the safe side. He didn't want to take that many, say forty or fifty tops. Now that was okay because Bobby'd only put half of them, or was it two thirds? — it was damn hard to tell — into the kettle. Call it two thirds. That meant there were probably a hundred and sixty in there. Fine, he'd drink a little less than the other lads and it'd work out perfectly. But what if the first cup had a greater concentration of mushrooms than the other two — maybe they'd all floated to the top. Or maybe they'd all sunk to the bottom, in which case it'd be better to go first. Fuck, Bachie thought, you're supposed to get paranoid *after* taking drugs. It had always been a little like this. Bobby, who was as impulsive as his hair, took everything with a nonchalant abandon; while Dewi always appeared so cocooned in his ample self as to be immune from any fear of excess — he could probably eat a whole field of mushies and not worry about it. It was only Bachie who ever got anxious and excited, the same way he'd got in the airport the one time he'd been abroad, breathlessly waiting to be elsewhere but a bit worried about leaving the ground.

Dewi drank the first cupful and went through a familiar after-drinking-mushrooms performance, which consisted of several seconds of pantomimic gagging and grimacing. Bachie went next. He always forgot how fucking awful they tasted. They were earthy and musty in his mouth, like he'd just lifted up an old rock and licked the ground beneath, sliding his tongue over squashed worms and slugs. His throat quivered as the last dregs of twiggy sludge went down. Bobby gulped down the remnants in the kettle and ran to the fridge to get a can of lager. And then they went out.

* * * *

As he walked past, Bachie looked at two old men who were sitting on one of the benches in the town square. It wasn't much of a square, just a bit of cobbled concrete with some benches, flanked on one side by a teashop and on the other by a pub. One of the men appeared to be vomiting into his hand. Bachie winced. And then he saw that the man was smiling at him, a broad, cheery, toothless grin, gums glistening, a pink tongue flicking between them like an iguana's. He was holding his teeth in his hand. The main road was full of people, most of them old. The smell of seaweed and rotting hung over them. Bobby stopped by the bus-stop outside Ena's Newsagents and was cornered by Mrs Roberts, one of his grandmother's friends, who was waiting there.

"Duw! Look at the size of you now Bobby," she said, even though Bobby wasn't that big at all. She was wearing thick red blusher, spread in uneven circles on her ancient, corrugated cheeks. Her face looked like cave paintings. She asked Bachie how his nain was. He said fine. She asked him to remember her to her when he saw her. He said he would. There were long white hairs on her chin; the longer he looked at them the longer they seemed to get. A car whooshed past on the road, fast at first but then slow as though it had suddenly driven underwater. The pavement appeared fluid and tremulous beneath his feet and in front of him a stop light was glaring red. A little girl went past, crying. He turned around and she was gone. Dewi was saying they should get to the pub. Bachie whispered to him that he was coming up.

Inside The George the air was stale and fusty, filled with a residue of old beer and perfume and cigarettes. Pubs, first thing in the day, always smelt like afterwards, the scent of what had been, quiet and still but musty with tumultuous memories. Pieces of brass shone dully above the empty fireplace. Some dogs played pool on the wall. Over in the corner were the noon regulars, smoking roll-ups and tearing up beer mats. Bobby asked him what he was drinking.

"I'll get the first round," said Bachie. Always best to get the first round, you never knew what state you'd be in later: get to the bar and panic and forget everyone's orders and look like an idiot.

Maureen, the barmaid, materialised behind the bar. Bright bottles of spirits were shining behind her — vodka and rum and whiskey, all sorts — refulgent, winking light through the room's dimness. Maureen's voice emerged through the scintillation, slow and gloomy in the twinkling, the blackness behind stars: "What can I get you Bachie?" She looked tired and sad and disappointed. She always did — it was the look of being leftover, and Maureen had always been left. She was beautiful at night beneath the barlights, but the daytime was cruel and it was always afterwards and they were always gone.

"Three lagers please, Maureen." Always best to keep it simple.

"What's Tracy up to today then?" she asked. Bachie detected a glimmer of revulsion, the hint of an accusation, in the words. He'd left her behind, at home with the kid, he was one of the leavers too. But how could he help it? Sit in that little house all day? The colour of headaches, the air thick with them. He didn't want to think about it, not now when he was tripping, when things should be different. Don't think. Why worry what this bitter old bitch thought.

"She's at her mother's."

Three pint glasses on the bar, cool and airy, bubbles drifting slowly in amber space. Dewi and Bobby were sitting in the corner by the fruit machine. Cherries and oranges pulsing through stale motes of dust. He carried all three at once to their table. Dewi was giggling and the noise seemed too small and feminine for his bulk. A strand of hair had fallen over his thin, meagre eyebrow. Bobby was telling how he'd shagged Cathy Giles, the wife of the bloke they all worked for at the moment, in the hayshed behind her house.

"Yea, so when was that you sly bastard," said Dewi.

"Yesterday," said Bobby. "Yesterday... and I knew she'd been wantin' to for ages, I'm tellin' yu... blind bastard 'asn't touched her for years... dragged me in there... tellin' yu —" "You're romancing the fucking stone mate... no fucking way... I was there yesterday —" "Not joking or nothing yeah... tellin' yu mate... dragged me in... hay an' all sorts everywhere —" "Bollocks... there... seen you...." Dewi's lips moving, small like a girl's. The words beginning to fade and fall apart, slowing and starting like lyrics on a twisted tape. Listening carefully, trying to hold them together as they oozed through the thick and sticky air. "...A bit porky an' everything..." "Bollocks —" "Got 'er eye on you as well Bachie, I reckon." In the hayshed, Cathy's arse in his hands, knicker elastic tugging against his wrists, fingers worming down through tangled fabric to reach backwards and below... coarse strands against the tips and then softness and the heat of wetness... a slight tightness giving way to slippery space. "Eye on you —" Smooth skin bunched and heavily breathing beneath him. Saliva smeared on his face. "...An' I don't think the bastard'd even care if he knew... probably just sits jerking himself off in his new tower." The sound of bleeping, rapid and hectic, cherries swirling, the colours throbbing now, aching against the window where the afternoon had crept slyly and hovered, murky and mysterious, behind the pane.

"I'm off for a piss," said Bachie, but no-one seemed to hear him, and so he stood up and went.

Inside the toilet it was cool and white. As he stood in front of the urinal it gurgled and retched, spewing water onto the blue cubes that nestled on the silver filter at the bottom; the water circled around them for a second and then slipped down into the dark slits in the silver. He reached inside his jeans and found he was semi-hard, a subtle tumescence that he hadn't even noticed — fuck, he'd just walked through the whole pub with a stiffie! Fuck, he was standing in the men's bogs with a hard-on! Best stop thinking of Cathy. He started thinking about Tracy. When was the last time? Ages, yes, ages now. Maybe it was the kid or something, always there, always. And when he tried to touch her the sense of crumpled slackness, of flesh somehow discarded and second-hand, something travelled through, exhausted — an old tyre left on the pavement, other people's breath. The first time afterwards a nightmare; thinking of it having been there, touching the sides with its soft, stubby little fingers, kicking out with tiny toes... couldn't stop thinking and her noticing how slow and tentative he was, seeing his awkward revulsion as delicacy (it was a bit, it was) — I'm not made out of bloody china now Bachie — what if there was blood too, leftover, covering him, out of sight in there, hot and sticky; imagining drowning in an underground cave, gulping down the dark and fetid water that had been there forever and never seen sunlight, and all the time the overwhelming desire for elsewhere, for anywhere. His piss arced in a yellowy-green parabola towards the blue cubes and ran away into the black gulf beneath the silver. The white tiles on the floor had begun flickering, like the edges of a film, and then to fall apart beneath his feet; the door of a cubicle tilted and swayed and then was still again for a second; everything seemed on the point of transformation and then was itself again and then.... In the mirror his face had become a pointillist portrait, colours dissolving into flecks and reforming into solid skin and dissolving once more. Got to get back.

Inside the bar it was different, as though he had been gone for eons (how long had he been gone?) as though time had moved on quicker here. It was crowded now, and noisy. The quiet dimness of noon had ignited into loud warm light; brass ornaments flamed on the walls, glasses shimmered and sparkled like liquid diamonds. The room was full of talking and laughing, a staccato cacophony that fell against his face like hailstones.

"Bachie... Bachie, mate." It was Dewi, his voice suddenly distinct through the stinging sound, his face looming through the giddy gleaming. It was good to see him. "We're off in a bit yea," he said, and then quieter, more confidential, "I'm fokked now Bachie, off my fokkin' cake." And then he smiled like it was their secret. And then he was gone and Bachie was looking at big Will Garage who was talking to him too, but he couldn't quite work out what he was saying but that was okay because he was smiling as he talked so Bachie smiled too. Will put a massive arm around his neck — there was a red and green snake that bulged on his bicep — and said to his companions "He's a good lad this one." Everyone agreed. Then he smiled some more and said something else that seemed to be a joke and rubbed his knuckles affectionately across Bachie's head. Everyone laughed. In the corner Bobby was motioning to him. A television screen had appeared over his head, bright blue with white writing growing rapidly out of a flickering cursor: Ar ...broath 0 C... owden ...beath 1, the writing multiplying swiftly and spreading down through the blue, eating away at its emptiness, until suddenly it had vanished and a man's face had appeared instead, talking, but there was no volume and he couldn't hear the words. Bobby pulled him down onto a seat: "There's your pint." Sat on the other side of the table were Sharon Mcqueen and Lisa Owen. Bobby was whispering something into Sharon's ear with laughing, lubricious lips.

"You're at it early Bachie," Lisa said, leaning towards him over the table. There were black feathers on the collar of her black coat, lustrous and bright. Her mouth was rosehip red. They'd gone to school together; she'd pinched his fags on the bus. "You coming to this party tonight?" she asked. He could smell lemons on her breath. He said yes and asked what party. She started laughing and said, "Well, I hope Bobby bloody knows 'cause he's taking us." Everything behind her was a confusion of movement and sound. Dewi, up at the bar, had dropped his pint on the floor. Maureen was having a go at him and Will was pointing and guffawing and Dewi, befuddled, looked as if it was all taking a bit to sink in. Lisa drew nearer, or so it seemed, and said, "Fuck, what's wrong with him?"

"He'll be a-right," Bachie replied, glad it wasn't him. Her breath was like lemonade.

* * * *

Outside it was night, cool and clear. The mushrooms had begun to wear off and had left behind a fuzzy, floating kind of drunkenness, like an afterthought. There was a thin sheen of old rain on the tarmac and as the cars went past their tyres cut through it and the sound was as gentle as an exhalation, soft and suspirious. Bachie felt himself relaxing. Ahead of him were Bobby and the girls, walking to where the main street slipped away under an arch to the seafront. Dewi was walking slightly behind him, cowed and silent after his mishaps. The streetlamps were shining and poured a sad orange light onto the pavement. Beneath the arch it was darker. There was a chippy on one side and through its windows Bachie could make out the spectral outline of a menu and shadowy glass shelves, hanging in the half-light, waiting for the day to ignite and fill them full of battered fish and pies. The whole shop was hushed, poised on the edge of a noisy tomorrow he somehow wished would never come. For a second he thought of his nain, stranded forever in a moment where nothing had really happened to her yet, where everything was about to happen but wouldn't because it already had; caught at the end of a life which she thought was about to begin. But the darkness under here was as small and swift as blinking and on the other side it opened out onto the straights, which looked vast and silver under the moonlight. Bachie followed the others towards the entrance of the pier. A cold but gentle breeze was blowing across the water and rocked the signs that advertised fishing and leisure trips; for eight pounds-fifty you could embark on the open sea — three times a day, pending weather conditions.

Bobby decided they should stop and have a smoke on the pier before leaving for the party, which had turned out to be miles off, on the mainland. Bachie hoped the delay would dampen their plans altogether. One hour ago Bobby had been struggling to find his way to the end of a sentence, the end of a road might be a big ask. Besides, what would he do if he couldn't get back by morning. She would be waiting for him. An empty chip wrapper scuttled like a paper crab across the street. He felt himself sobering up and the world slowing down. Out here there was only the still light and the sluggish sound of the sea. Through the windows of the Bulkely Hotel, whose terrace looked out on the water, he could see people in the bar, soundlessly talking and laughing, encased behind glass as if they were an exhibit in a museum, mute and sealed away; they seemed inconceivably remote, as far away as memory. There were times when he wished he could get as far away from his own life, that he could look at it through windows. But what magic could take him that far?

Persistence

If he hadn't seen her name it would have all been fine. He certainly would never have come to this place — although he still wasn't exactly sure why he had come or what he would do now that he had arrived or what could possibly be accomplished by his presence. Old men should let sleeping dogs lie, or was that dead dogs? Leave resurrections to Lazarus and his like. Why hope to resuscitate what he wished dead. If only he hadn't seen her name. But of course in a way he had been looking for it all along, searching through the pages of the newspaper as persistently and plaintively as those abandoned lovers in old ballads, their eyes fixed on the horizon, waiting and wailing on the shore for their lost and sea-tossed paramours. But he could hardly have expected to find it. The looking was one thing, an unhealthy reflex — something like hope, but more like the twitch of a phantom limb, the visceral commemoration of an absence. The looking was predicated on the not finding, on the never finding. Why else did he only read the island paper, where no one would ever have expected her to be, certainly not him. And then suddenly there she was: nestled in between the picture of a school band once again triumphant in an Eisteddfod — always the same story, the same picture, only different faces sometimes, if you bothered to look — and a bull who had triumphed in the Anglesey show; hidden amongst those very items that for forty years or more had comforted him with the idea that here — in *The Anglesey Mail* at least — the world was a simple and timeless succession of smiling schoolchildren and bulky, bovine champions, that here at least the places where she lived and moved were as distant and indistinct as Plutonian moons. And then there she was, her name close-up in black and white, the ink recalling her from lunar vastness — an otherworldly intrusion, an alien invasion. The familiar feel of his heart swelling and splintering.

Of course they called it a homecoming. Famous lady comes back to her roots for a swansong. After the name, the details had shuddered in front of him like aftershocks: *Megan Jones, the internationally renowned artist, returns to her native Anglesey this week to attend the opening of an exhibition of her work at the Oriel Gallery. Megan, who was born and raised in....* No need to carry on, he knew very well, where and when and how long. But how strange to see her translated into sentences, a succession of words in which he was only an ellipsis, a gap between letters; and other lines, further on, in which he was not even a lacunae, lines in which she had lived in other places and been married and divorced and had children and become old and reduced him to a memory, if that.

* * * *

It was, without any doubt whatsoever, the worst moment imaginable to bump into Mrs Evans, the councillor's wife. She was standing in the entrance to the gallery, wearing a dress full of flowers, and by the time he realised it was her, there was no getting away. He watched with infinite gloom as her eyes lit up in recognition.

"Hello Jack," she said (everyone else called him Cucu), "fancy seeing you here."

She had been Mrs Evans for nigh on thirty years now and cultivated and encouraged this august moniker, as befitting her status as one of the first ladies of the borough. Cucu, who had pulled her pigtails in the playground, reached back for the name that predated her giddy social elevation: "Hello Delyth."

Mrs Evans frowned, ever so slightly.

"Well, who would have thought it," she said, "our Megan — famous and everything — back home. Who would have thought it. I still remember us playing together in school, best friends we were, back then of course."

Megan, as Jack recalled, had also pulled Mrs Evans' pigtails; often they had done it together, one each, until her blubbering had got them a cane on the hand from the teacher. "And you two courting afterwards, when we were older. Now there's one you let slip Jack — what with all these paintings she must be a rich woman now. You should've got a ring on her finger while you had the chance."

Jack wished there was a way he could crack open the pavement and uncover some cavernous rift in the earth, into which he could push Mrs Evans, listening as her voice receded into the immeasurable oblivion. But that didn't seem to be an option and so he did what he had done best for forty years now, whenever someone had brought Megan up in conversation, or even someone who wasn't her but happened to share her name, he stayed absolutely silent, until the other person became awkward and left either him or the subject behind. Unfortunately, silence was a poor defence against the assaults of Mrs Evans: "...No need for you to keep on running after those sheep and cows, eh Jack, and a big house in London I'm sure and..." Jack improvised with a new technique: "I'm sorry Delyth, but I really must get to the toilet."

Inside the cubicle he struggled to pluck away the stray threads that had begun to sprout, quite alarmingly, from the sleeves of his jacket. It had been a long time since he had needed to think what he should wear anywhere. Since formality was not at a premium in the fields, and, down at The Dragon, wellies and oilskins were still very much the vogue, there had been little need to worry about wardrobes. Looking for his best outfit he had discovered that he only really had his funeral clothes, a suit of shiny black cloth whose long stints of sombre duty in the island's graveyards had begun to affect it in a quite material fashion. Standing by the gallery entrance earlier, where he had waited for several hours — wondering at the folly of this visit, unable once again, like her, to just walk away — he had watched a pastoral procession of vivid flowers walk past, pink roses and petunias, buttercups and daisies, floating by on beds of cotton and fields of muslin, as though each visitor were a celebrant in some vernal pageant, and, looking down at his old, lugubrious costume, he had felt like he was bringing coffins to a maypole.

* * * *

Once upon a time the suit had been new: when his father came back from Denbigh dead; an inverted resurrection, since he had gone there alive. You've got to look your best, his mother had said when she presented it to him, as though his father might be somehow disappointed if he didn't, frowning down from eternity, or wherever he had gone, at his son's negligent attire. His father though, it must be said, looked impeccable on his return. Pillowed between the red velvet cushions, his wedding suit ironed sheer and brushed spotless, his shoes buffed and beaming, and within them his corpse laid out with such a stiff formality, such a military straightness, that he looked as if, when the final reckoning arrived and God's great bugle sounded, he would rise effortlessly to attention, without a single button out of place. Of course he had always been an exceptionally well-kempt and tidy man, almost excessively so. And maybe it was this outward fastidiousness that had made his inward unravelling seem so terrible.

Because who could have known, that day they first saw him — for young Jack the first time quite literally (he had been born the week after his father left and almost grown up without ever seeing him) — returned at last from the fighting, walking down the lane dressed in a uniform that would have had any sergeant major in the world swooning, his short hair bryl-creamed into a glistening, black coronet, his face shaved to an almost cherubic softness. Who could have known the awful mess he had brought back with him, hidden within his perfectly presented skull? There was no way of telling. And to begin with there was nothing to tell. Jack, who had suddenly got a father and, to tell the truth, was not absolutely sure if this was quite the boon everybody else made out it was — he had been kicked out of his mother's bed and replaced by a stranger — saw nothing at all amiss.

And then came the nightmares and the fevers. Together at first, as though one were the adjunct of the other, a set of concomitant afflictions that flared up intermittently and seemed to feed each off the other. There were long days and nights, his father shivering and screaming, not knowing the darkness from the light; his mother's eyes pinched and desperate but not hopeless, not yet. Because, to begin with, it would pass. After a few days, a week sometimes, his father would rise from his bed, his skin shrunken and yellow but his eyes bright again, in the world again, and together they would go about as though this time it was gone for good, as though this time the island breezes had ushered away whatever dread incubus had secreted itself into his brain. They had a name for it then too, malaria, which made it seem less terrible, more familiar, something that, as Dr Roberts assured Jack's mother, all the boys seemed to have brought back with them from Burma. It was only a fever. A bug in the blood his dad called it, trying to explain to his son that the things he saw when he was sick were only there because of what he had brought back in his veins, that though his body was corrupted his mind and eyes were fine. But the bug just seemed to get stronger and stronger, and after a few years it no longer appeared to need a whole body to afflict. The shivers went, and the sweating too, but the nightmares grew and multiplied, edging the world out of his irises, congealing beneath his eyelids, turning everything into one long and febrile hallucination.

* * * *

It was about this time that Jack fell in love with Megan, if ten year olds can fall in love. They lived next door to each other, more or less. Jack's house, a white farmhouse, was etched into the side of a hill which rose on one side directly out of the granite-black and froth-flecked cliffs that guarded the island's eastern shore, and, on the other, fell away into the undulating, maternal mosaic of fields that spread inward and westward. Megan's place, a small, tidy cottage, lay at the end of the track that led to Jack's, sitting like a gatehouse to some grander building, looking up at it, watching it. Each day, after school, they would walk back together, stopping at Megan's house for her mother's tea and cakes, before clambering towards Jack's to play on the hill. Its sides were spotted with oaks and beach and sycamore, that nestled together to form tall, arched, secluded sanctuaries, surrounded by the distant thump of wave on rock and the curlew's callings. On its summit the trees had shrunk into hawthorn shrubs and blackthorn bushes, their branches gnarled and spiky like the ends of a witch's broom, the wind screeching through them. The hill was an entire world, with secret places and strange populations, with histories and mythologies all of its own. There were fairies and goblins and a fox with one leg missing whom Megan stole loaves of stale bread for; there was a raven called Branwen who, Megan assured Jack, was a very tragic figure; there was a heap of stones where smugglers had lived and a man had been murdered by his own brother.

On the top of the hill stood an old windmill, surrounded by

wild roses, with tendrils of ivy creeping up its crumbling, white walls; its sails, drooping like broken wings, still clinging, half-shattered, to its front, leaving wind-shorn shards of wood to moulder on the ground amongst the nettles and the rose thorns. In the daytime it was a place of endless fascination. Someone, many years before, had kicked the door open and left it ajar. Inside was a mysterious stillness, materialised in silent motes of ancient flour dust, magnified by the presence of stationary objects of movement — winches and pulleys and shoots and great round mill stones — all left eerily static in the pale beams of immobile light that filtered through the dusty windows. Old grain sacks lay scattered on the floor, crumpled and forgotten, sprouting grass in the springtime. A miller's white smock hung quietly from one of the rafters. At first, when the two of them entered, they felt cowed and tentative, as though even their breath might prove too much a disturbance for the place, a reckless, eddying wind in the face of which the whole building would vaporise and vanish, leaving them standing on the empty hilltop. Yet, after a while, they would become more bold, assimilating the abandoned interior into the world of the hill, where it became their faery citadel, their house, their tower, a Camelot all to themselves. But only in the daytime; because, as the light began to fade, and the evening breeze came soughing through the sail blades, and the seagulls returning from the sea shrieked through the air, and the shadows came crawling out of the corners, they would remember the stories told about the tower and the miller. There was nothing definite — their mothers and fathers said that he had just gone — only pieces of stories, fragments you picked up here and there. They said he had gone crazy and killed a woman, before throwing himself from the top of the tower; they said he'd had his heart broken by a woman and cut his throat, leaving a stream of blood congealed on the building's walls; they said that at night his ghost still worked the mill, and sometimes, when the moon was bright, you could see the sails revolving in its light. And, as the darkness came, and these fragments came once more to life, they would scuttle out and run down towards the lights of their houses, holding hands against the terrors of the night.

They were seldom apart. Soon they began to wander past the edges of the hill. Crossing its summit, they clambered down its far side, towards a narrow lane that led to the sea. Opposite, on an adjacent rise, was the house of Idris Llewelyn, who had been with Jack's father in Burma. Sometimes his wife, watching from her kitchen, glassy discs in front of her eyes, would wave at them. Sometimes their dog, a vicious young puppy called Carlo, would bound across the fields in their direction, slavering and snarling, and they'd have to start running. Though it was no more than a mile from where they lived it was like being in another country; each twist in the lane was a border crossing. Halfway to the sea they found a little cottage with two windows in its front that looked like cat's eyes. One of them had ivy growing across it and when they went past the cottage it looked as if it was giving them a lazy, feline wink. A foreign man lived in the place, called Joe the Baker, because he baked little cakes and loaves and went around on a rickety bicycle selling them. Once they'd walked past his house a couple of times he started running out to greet them, materialising suddenly at his back gate like a benign gnome, holding a small tray full of cakes and currant buns. He had a big round ruddy face and a wide smile, that he'd push towards them along with his tray, saying "Cake, cake", which was all he'd say because he didn't speak any more of their languages. But he spoke quite enough with his smile, which twinkled and laughed and joked, and they'd pocket the cakes and say thank you and he'd smile some more and say "Cake" and wave them on their way. Jack asked his father how Joe the Baker had got here.

"He's a refugee," said his father.

"Is that someone from Germany?" asked Jack, because the only foreigners he'd seen who weren't English were the German prisoners who'd worked in their fields during the war.

"No, he's someone who lost their home in the war. Joe's Polish, from Poland."

"Did you fight against Poland?"

"No, we fought with it, for it."

"Is that why he gives me cakes?"

"He gives you cakes because he's a nice man," said his father.

Further down the lane, near the cliff tops, there was a small house where a witch lived. They knew she was a witch because she was old and had wild red hair that fell in withered curlicues across her face and that, according to Megan, was what witches looked like. They spent hours spying on her, painfully and breathlessly hidden in thick, prickly gorse bushes whose yellow flowers smelt like the white insides of the coconuts that Jack's father had brought home from the fair once. They watched as she roamed the strip of moorland, called Y Fedw, that stretched out behind her house and down to the sea; it was blanketed in heather and gorse, stunted willows and scraggly birches, and became purple and yellow and orange and white as the seasons turned and changed. Jack thought she might only be gathering firewood, but Megan assured him she was collecting herbs, roots and poisonous berries to make potions. When they knew she was out gathering, they snuck as close as they dared to the windows of the house; inside dead babies hung from the low wooden beams, swirling in the updrafts of warm air that seeped out from an old aga that was as black as burnt corpses. Sometimes the dead babies looked like bags of onions, or dried flowers, or ragged dolls, but they could never quite pluck up the courage to get a closer view. The witch kept a little vegetable garden in her front yard and Megan said that witches planted dead babies in their gardens to grow mandrake roots; a fact which Jack was happy to agree with, even though he wasn't entirely sure what a mandrake root was — presumably something that grew into a man. Jack asked his mum about the witch.

"Good heavens!" she said. "That's poor Mrs Edwards."

"When did she start being a witch?" Jack asked. At which point his dad had come into the room and said, "About fifty-five years ago by my reckoning."

"Stop it, the pair of you," his mum blustered. "Poor Mrs Edwards isn't any witch, she's a widow and has to make do all on her own."

"What's a widow?"

"It's someone who's lost their husband. And a terrible tragedy it was for Mrs Edwards, to lose hers so young."

"Megan says she plants dead babies in the garden to grow man roots. Is she doing that to get a new husband?"

In the corner of the room his father held a hand to his mouth and started snorting.

"Well, she's got quite an imagination, that girl," said his mum a bit disapprovingly, as though this was something rather distasteful. "You'll do well not to believe every word she tells you."

If it rained and it was too wet to go on the hill, or anywhere else, Megan made them play husband and wife in the haybarn behind Jack's house. When it was full you could make tunnels and rooms in the bales, a whole Cretan underworld full of twisting turns and musty halls of dry grass. They made a kitchen and living room and a bedroom. They'd make jam butties in the kitchen, fumbling with old loaves and a silver, serrated knife Jack had stolen from his mother's cutlery drawer. Then, scrambling on elbows and knees, they carried them through the snug passages that led into the living room, where they'd sit and eat, pulling the occasional strand of hay from between their teeth and giggling in the dusty half-light. Afterwards, Megan would begin yawning in an exaggerated, slightly comical way, stretching her arms above her head, and say, "Okay, it's time for bed," even though it was only afternoon. She'd take him by the hand then and pull him through into the darkest and smallest of the rooms. Inside the air seemed thicker and hotter, like the air beneath a blanket. For a while they would just lie there, side by side, with pieces of sharp straw jutting into their backs and fragments of dried buttercup falling onto their faces. And then Megan would begin to shift and fidget, squirming impatiently in the gloom, her breath quickening and pulsing through the dead pollen that hung in the heavy air.

"We have to be proper husbands and wives," she'd say at

last. "You know, and do things." But Jack wasn't too sure what things he was supposed to do.

"What things?"

"You know, touch each other and things," but he still wasn't sure what things.

"Here," she'd say, and grab his hand, pushing it none too delicately beneath her blouse, "feel them." So he'd move his fingers over her chest, which felt like his own, brushing them over the soft skin and the little nipples that stood out like goose bumps. He could hear the rain pattering on the corrugated tin of the roof, loud and lonely, like the only noise in the world. Afterwards, when they climbed out of the barn, the light made him blink, and the air tasted like fresh water.

* * * *

Away from the hill and the barn there was his father, whose nightmares had begun to creep into the daylight. The first time it was Jack that found him. He was meant to be fixing a wall in one of their bottom fields and Jack's mother had given him a batch of corn beef sandwiches to deliver to him while he was working. Jack took them and walked down towards the field, looking across at the weathered slab of Ynys Seiriol and, beyond it, the forlorn expanse of the Orme, thinking how strange it was that men had chosen to live in such places once, with nothing but salt water and stone for company. He followed the long line of the wall that dipped and rose with the contours of the pale green ground, before falling like a tear towards the sea. It was late autumn and the sea had turned a chilly purple; cold cloud shadows swept across the water, making their melancholy way towards the horizon. Jack's father was lying beneath two sycamores whose branches were entwined like lovers over the top of the wall.

"Get down," his father said, in a harsh, hissed whisper. Jack didn't know what to do so he bent down beside him. His father grabbed the collar of his coat and pulled him flat onto the wet grass.

"Are you trying to get yourself killed?" he said. "They know our position."

"Who, dad?" Jack asked. But his father said nothing and it was then that Jack knew his father was not seeing him at all, that, in his father's eyes, he was no more than a cipher in some tormented landscape that would not let him go, that would not let him come home. They lay on the ground together for about an hour. Jack's father had given him a small carved elephant that he'd brought back from the war and he tried to imagine what a real one would look like, lumbering over these fields, picking ivy with his trunk from the tops of oak trees, stepping over stone walls and sleeping in the haybarn. He tried to conjure up the tigers his father had told him about, and the snakes as long as five men; he tried to see the palm trees and jungles and the rivers spotted with giant buffaloes that lived in the water. But in the end, as the wind dropped shrivelled orange leaves onto his head, and the lonely cloud shadows moved farther away into the north and the west and the wetness of the grass made him shiver, all he could see was another cold autumn day on the island and the tired, frightened man beside him.

At one point his father glanced nervously behind him, towards where the tower stood looking down on them from the top of the hill.

"If they take the lookout then we're done for!" he said.

But despite Jack's father's ever more assiduous efforts, they kept on taking the lookout. However watchful he remained, however long and vigilantly he stood sentinel before it, however bravely he kept to his position, they would, in the end, overrun it. At the conclusion of each defeat he would rush back into the house, usually dressed in only a pair of khaki trousers (his elegance trounced once more on the battlefield) and a vest, whatever the weather, his face and arms camouflaged with thick smears of black mud, twigs and leaves entangled in his hair. It was an odd sort of retreat, past the bubbling pans on the aga, around trays of newly baked bread, but on he would go, through the warm, doughy air, careering towards the small, dark room at the back of the house where they kept the coal and which he had taken as his final place of refuge. Then he would be gone, because nobody could open the door or even speak to him; all they could do was wait. Sometimes it was only for an evening, sometimes it was whole days and nights, but, eventually, he would come back, impeccable in tweed, his brylcream gleaming, looking exactly as he had on the day of his first return, ready to take up again the life he had left behind.

But he stayed less and less. Month by month, week by week, the repetitive drama of defence and defeat and retreat began to subsume even these brief periods of respite. It was as though his disease worked by way of contraction and concentration, squeezing his waking world — God only knew what lurked in his sleeping one — into the confines of one small, inescapable realm of memory, a place whose contours and landscape they didn't know, and couldn't know, but which had converted everything into its own image. Because disease it was, though by now they knew it was no bug in the blood, no malaria, nothing some little insect could insert and a man could sweat out. Dr Roberts couldn't tell them what it was; he didn't have a name that would fit or comfort anymore. No one else had come back with this. And it didn't work like any disease he had seen before; it was like some crazed and dementedly reductive dramatist who slashed up men's scripts and burnt down their stages and left them with one scene, one act, one single passage, that they were cursed to play out again and again and forever.

People began to take it for granted. When other farmers came around they would delicately ask where he was, and if the reply was the coal room, then they would make their polite apologies and leave — there was no longer any need for explanations. Idris, who lived over the hill, began to come over quite often. Jack's mother hoped there was something he could do. He tried to talk to him; he sat for hours outside the coal room door; he even lay down beside him in the fields and shared his long watches. But whatever it was that they had shared once, it was not this. Jack listened behind the kitchen door to Idris and his mother talking, the one desperate, the other sad and hopeless: "There must be something, Idris, you were with him; there must be something that happened to him, something we can help?"

"There were lots of things that happened over there, Gwen,

lots of terrible things. But he won't talk to me, it's like I'm not even there."

"But there must be something, something you can do?"

"He doesn't talk to me, Gwen. I don't think he even hears me."

"But you were there together Idris, it happened to both of you, you came back together."

"I don't think he has come back, Gwen, I don't think he has. God help the poor bugger."

Afterwards Jack's mother didn't talk much, not to Jack, not to Idris, not to anybody. She walked around in a kind of daze, slow and unblinking, every movement mechanical and methodical; an automaton in a skirt to go with the madman in khaki. Jack found out his father had a new name. He was coming home from school, past the church, when he came across a couple of men hacking the tops off the hedges with long, curved scythes. He didn't recognize them but they seemed to know him. One of them turned his head through a flurry of falling twigs and said to the other: "That's Cucu's lad, isn't it?" But his companion only arched his eyebrows to let him know that Jack could hear him, and then, when he realised it was too late to stop him hearing, turned to Jack and said, "Send our best to your father now." And Jack walked on, wondering who they were but knowing there was nobody left for him to ask.

Things couldn't have got worse, and then they did. His father began carrying a gun with him on his patrols. It wasn't much of a gun — just a rusty old blunderbuss sort of thing that they'd used once or twice to shoot magpies behind the house — and certainly seemed a poor and ineffective aid in the quest to hold the lookout;

but gun it was, and for those in the neighbourhood who were sympathetic towards the plight of Cucu, it was seen as an ominous development in his campaign. By this time, Jack's mother had retreated so far into her robotic silence that the appeals of various concerned visitors quickly became inquiries into her own health. Jack made a few abortive attempts to steal the gun and hide it, but his father's madness was as alert as a hawk now and protected its new toy with unflagging attentiveness. Maybe, if he had stayed on his own land, they might have delayed things. But he didn't. As his world got smaller and smaller, the battlefield kept getting bigger. Idris found him behind his pigpen. Mrs Edwards came visiting to tell them he wouldn't leave her garden. Finally, one May evening, two men walked up the track with Jack's father between them, naked and soaking and smeared with mud. Jack watched them approach the door. They weren't smiling. As soon as his mother answered their knock his father broke out of their grasp and dashed towards the coal room, globs of wet earth falling from his bare buttocks. They'd found him in the river beside The Dragon, pointing his gun at the short bridge that led into the car park. They spoke to his mother for a long time but she didn't seem to be listening, and when Jack asked what they had said she wouldn't speak to him. They came for him the very next week.

Jack remembered the van coming up the drive, clunking over potholes, wreathes of dust trailing its wheels. He remembered Dr Roberts standing in the yard looking tired and sad, and Idris beside him. There were two other men but he didn't know them. He remembered the smell of coconuts and honeysuckle. It was Idris who had gone inside to fetch him. He led him outside, holding him around the shoulders like he was a child. Dr Roberts was with his mother. One of the strangers came up to Jack and ruffled the hair on his head and said not to worry, that he'd be taken care of. And then the van was leaving and they were gone and his mother had begun crying, muffled at first but then loud, so loud that he wanted to put his hands over his ears. He watched as the van began to disappear around the corner of the drive, staring at a shape that he could make out through its back window, a shape that he thought was his father. The war, or one small piece of it, had lasted longer than his life.

* * * *

One year later he said goodbye to Megan, which was worse. Her father, a merchant seaman, had got a desk job in London and was taking his family away with him. At first she was inconsolable and then, in a few weeks, she was a bit excited. By now they were fourteen years old and lovers. Megan said not to worry, that she'd be back every summer, that if she hated it down there — which she assured him she would — then she would run away and come live with him, that maybe they could get married and live on his farm which, by now, he'd left school to work on because his father had been taken away. And, because it was May again, and the fields were yellow with buttercups and the sea looked warm and the hedges smelt of flowers, they believed that this might happen, that it would. But it didn't. The first winter there were long letters, saying how awful things were, how she missed him and the island

and hated London and her father. She said she would see through the winter, but after that she'd come back and there was nothing anybody could do to stop her. But she went to France that summer, because her father was a tyrant and made her go. Then he began to get postcards instead of letters. They had famous paintings on them. The writing on the back said she missed him. Then the writing stopped saying that she missed him and was full of the names of the places she'd been to. Jack bought an old atlas and looked them up and couldn't imagine what they were like to be in. The next winter there were two letters, one at Christmas, full of people and places he didn't know. And then there were no letters or postcards. Apart from one.

It must have been five years later, because he'd just turned twenty-one. It was a postcard. His mother left it on the table for him and he knew straight away that it was from her because it had a picture on it. The picture was of a Polynesian girl, wrapped in a white cloth, who was looking, slightly sadly, into a distance the picture didn't contain. Jack felt a bit embarrassed that his mother had seen it. On the back she said how bad it was that they'd lost touch with each other. She said that she was at art school now and was coming back to the island for a few weeks to do some sketching. She asked if he'd like her to visit while she was around. There was an address scrawled in the corner but he didn't bother to look at it, because he didn't want her to visit him, not after he'd spent this long trying not to think about her, trying to whittle away the memory of her until it had become a bag of dry and insubstantial bones, ready at last to be buried and forgotten. He didn't know then how long they would persist, how long the flesh would cling to them. For a month she was everywhere. Everyone he knew or saw, or so it seemed, had met her. Old men who never left their land had posed for her; reclusive widows came bustling into the lanes; if there had still been solitary saints and anchorites living on the island he was sure they would have invited her in. She was as ubiquitous as April rain. He lived in dread and hope of bumping into her, prepared his speeches, went through all possible conversations, gathered himself together before each turn in every road, ready to look surprised and outraged and angry all at once. But she was beyond none of them. And then she was gone. He didn't know it would be for forty years and more. He didn't know how long he'd miss her.

* * * *

It looked almost like it had looked, back then: the sails silent and half fallen, the walls intact, the whitewash crumbling, the door still ajar — mysterious, inviting. But the light was different. It was brighter, more luminous, as though memory had intensified the sunbeams and cleared the skies; drying up the dampness and the drizzle, pushing the rain shadows away beyond the framed horizon. Maybe it was the paint she used? Thick, glossy oils embossed on a watercolour world. Or maybe this was just how she saw it, or had seen it? All serene and sun baked, flooded with nothing but kind light. The hill had become a mound of green heaped onto the canvas, with only the strokes of the brush visible in its undergrowth. His house was a blotch of white in the background. The haybarn was gone. Everything in the picture seemed so still: the colours as glazed and static as glass, the lines etched and dead, the brush marks nothing but memorials of long-forgotten movements, like the dry and whorled bed of some evaporated sea. She'd called it The Tower.

Other people came crowding past him. Mostly the women wearing flowers who had, by now, added some interested smiles to their outfits and stopped here and there to stare into the sun-washed precincts of the picture. They all seemed to like it and said so in polite whispers. He looked across the wall, into the other frames. Several old men looked back at him, wearing shabby jackets and flat caps, their obsidian eyes peering out from chapped, red faces. They all had titles, some anonymous, some with names, some he remembered: Farmer: Llanddona, 1959; Idris Evans, cattle trader: Llangefni Market, 1959; Joe, baker: 1959. He tried once again to pluck the frayed threads from his sleeves and then looked back into their mute faces, but all he saw now was a gallery of corpses; a collection of peasant emblems and rustic icons, all salt of the earth, enduring like stars though they were as dead as dodos. He sensed how much they were like the tower, semblances caught in a light that was not properly their own, that shone backwards into a world where it didn't belong and could never exist. Turning to go he realised that she had still not come back, that these people and these places were from a dead time which she had never left, and that he had never let go.

Of Rocks and Stones

It was late in January and the Reverend Edward Morris was sitting at the desk in his study, watching through his window as successive banks of cloud swooped in from the sea, slowing to crawl over the Orme and Ynys Seiriol, before stopping momentarily to lower over his roof and deposit their seemingly bottomless supply of rain upon it. The wind that drove them was veering uncertainly, sending the waves below first this way and then that, churning the surface of the water into a blizzard of baffled white crests. This time of year he tended to take the weather personally — everyone did. There was always an edge in January to what might otherwise seem merely perfunctory observations about climatic conditions — a feeling that their malignity was aimed directly at you, was summoned for the specific purpose of wearing down your already frayed spirit, to make sure that before spring came you would be well and truly beaten. Conversations about the weather in January were a perilous business, Morris had realised, because there was always a hint of blame directed against him, as though somehow he were complicit in it, had worked it all out with the creator he was supposed to represent as a cruel test of faith. He could see it in their eyes, the suspicion. And there was nothing he could do to dispel it, because whatever mysterious ways impelled these clouds to descend like the lid of a cauldron in November and remain until May, he was not able to explain, or indeed justify them, to men. Besides, he was a victim of it as much as they were, and took his place each season in the assembled ranks of island Jobs.

He'd spent the morning trying to write a letter to his brother in America. He attempted this at least once a year, invariably at some point in mid-winter. So far he'd completed two in ten years, but had never sent any. What actually compelled him to begin them in the first place remained something of an enigma to him. He had not seen or spoken to his brother, who taught geography in a college somewhere in Florida (he had not quite reached the point of memorising an address), for ten years or more, which was an awfully long time — long enough, certainly, to explain his compulsion as guilt. But it didn't feel like guilt. There were just days when the ring of mountains and sea outside his window began to tighten slightly, an infinitesimal contraction, but one that made him restless and fidgety as though he were chafing against some invisible constraint. And then, almost without willing it, he would find himself here at his desk, pen in hand, scribbling to a brother he had nigh on forgotten, not really knowing what he was saying or why he was saying it. In return for his unfinished letters, he received, at Christmas, a page written by his brother's American wife, describing what "we" had done this year, a collective pronoun that included their two sons, a Labrador and two cats; sometimes he was interested in what the cats had done, but only sometimes.

Today's letter today had begun quite gloomily — how could he help it with half the Irish Sea cascading down his drain pipes and the rest, apparently, sweeping in from the grey horizon — in a style he feared was a bit stilted and self-indulgent (his brother had little time for flowery prose, he had always preferred bold, uncluttered lines that did not deviate as they passed over the terrain beneath: longitudes, latitudes). Dear William, it began

Another long winter to suffer through. The rectory has decided to let in more of God's breath this year, which sweeps through the rooms with all the desolate aplomb of an Old Testament lament. Or perhaps these draughts are just the ghosts of chilly sermons past, come back from the deceased mouths of my predecessors to haunt me. All this must seem very remote to you these days, ensconced, as I imagine you to be, on a pleasant porch, swathed in tropical sunshine and drinking mint juleps. I doubt you can have too many regrets about leaving — there was so little for you here. I think about you often (sometimes) though. Yesterday I walked to the beach down past Cucu's place, the one with the white stones (I suppose it's all white sand over there), to look at the rock pools we used to catch shrimps in when we were boys. They have hardly changed at all, although the beach itself is a bit different. The council, or the National Trust, I can't be sure which, has built a car park at the top of the cliff and the old path that went down through the ferns has been replaced by a fancy new track made of wood and gravel. There are more people too, mainly fishermen from Liverpool, and more rubbish; mostly plastic bags, that hang like a foul drapery off the orange bracken. I actually tried to catch a few shrimps but they easily eluded me (I'm not quite so sprightly as I was back then), and instead grazed my hand on a very ancient looking limpet, which was itself encrusted with barnacles, as though it had been there for so long that it had become mistaken for the rock it clung to. I wondered if it had been there since we were children, if maybe it had grazed me before. I know it might sound odd, but afterwards I felt a certain affinity with this old limpet, clinging for a whole lifetime to one small piece of rock, in one small pool, on one small beach. Because haven't I, in a way, been doing exactly the same thing? Yes, of course, my Rock may well be larger — in both a spiritual and geographical sense — but isn't it possible that my horizons have perhaps been correspondingly bounded, that I have looked up at the surface of my pool, through the water darkly, and imagined I looked on the whole world, when all the time I was straining my eyes to glimpse only the merest fragment of it. I have never been married, I have never had children, I have never lived anywhere but here on this small island that lies beside a small country off the coast of a small continent. And yet....

And yet what, he thought, pausing with his pen and looking down over the broad expanse of white that remained below the ink. Outside the window a cloud had stopped on the opposite shore of the straits and lay, exhausted, beneath the round summit of Carnedd Dafydd. He put his pen down on the desk, picked up the piece of paper, and was just on the point of depositing it in the bin when a knock on the door diverted him. It was Gwynfor Owen, who owned the garage in the village. He had obviously come straight from work and there were smears of black oil on his forehead and cheeks; droplets of rain clung to his silver hair and occasionally fell down onto his face, slithering off the oil and sliding down his neck. He looked as though coming to the Reverend Morris's house was the last thing he would have chosen to do and that this visit had weighed heavily upon him for the whole morning. There were pinched, determined creases at the corners of his eyes. It took a while for him to speak, which was not unusual because Gwynfor didn't like to speak much, and when he did, each utterance was short and blurted, spluttering rapidly into silence like a faulty car ignition.

"Sorry to bother you Mr Morris."

"Not at all, Gwynfor. What can I do for you?"

"It's Catrin. I wondered if you'd come by and see her."

"That's no problem, Gwynfor, but why does she want to see me?"

"She's not herself."

"What, you mean she's sick? Have you got the doctor around yet?"

"It's not like that, Mr Morris."

Morris was about to ask how it was then exactly, or what it was at least, but Gwynfor was quite evidently at the very limit of his conversational reserves — the strained creases beside his eyes were deepening into rifts and canyons — and so he just said fine, he'd come around first thing in the evening.

As he watched Gwynfor walk back towards his car a gust of wind rippled over the confused waters of the straits, lifting up the resting cloud and driving it onwards, where it shattered on the peaks of Foel Coch and Mynydd Perfedd.

* * * *

As the darkness began to fall the sky became clearer and the wind became colder. He walked along the road that led from the old priory and Seiriol's well into the village. The waves, which by now had steadied themselves and found their true direction, lashed the sea wall to his left, sending clumps of chilly foam rolling across the tarmac. He made his way around to where the road touched the edge of Traeth Lleiniog, where spectral cliffs of sandstone crumbled into the sea, leaving strange shaped remnants beached on the shore. A pale and sodden moon heaved itself above the adjacent mountains and then vanished as he moved beneath the branches of the glen. Here a path opened up through the trees and he took it, lifting his feet carefully over the knotted, Gordian roots that sprawled across the ground in the shadows. To his surprise he found himself still speaking to his brother

And yet isn't it also true that sometimes the most limited vantage point offers the widest view? You do not need to stand on the summit of Pisgah to see the world. A hard point to make nowadays, I know, when everyone, or so it seems, has travelled to the four corners of it. Whenever I talk to my parishioners they are always recounting the peripatetic exploits of restless sons, daughters and grandchildren, toing and froing from places I have only ever seen in photographs in that heap of National Geographics in the dentist's waiting room. But when they come back are they not still as young as I was at their age? You can have memories of the entire globe and very little understanding of any of it. The limpet never moves an inch but, over time, whole oceans will wash over it. Do you remember....

His foot stopped suddenly, though he did not remember willing it to stop, and the rest of his body had not seemed to make the necessary adjustment, its momentum pushing over it and heaving itself onto the muddy ground. One of the roots had downed him. He lay there for a second, looking up at the branches above him and the sky beyond them, seeing blackness etched across darkness.

His ankle was hurt, there was no doubt about it, but how badly hurt he wasn't sure. It still moved, a good sign. He was amazed that he'd fallen. How many times had he walked this way, during the day and the night. He'd thought he knew each obstacle, or at least that his feet did. It should have been instinct by now. He felt somehow betrayed — by his feet, by the track. But there was nothing else to do but hobble on, and so he did, until finally two orange lights appeared in front of him. As he approached them the track merged once more into tarmac and the branches receded into thin, umbrageous wisps. Houses began to take shape alongside of him and he could make out the weak lights that spread through forlorn, January kitchens, which everyone had vacated to hide around living room fires and the comforting glow of televisions, where palm trees swayed and people had skin as soft and clear as peaches. Soon he'd arrived beneath the streetlamps that stood like sentinels at the bottom of the road leading up the hill through the village. Just beyond the pools of sad orange that oozed onto the ground around them, he could make out a small group of children huddled around the bus shelter, hiding precious cans of lager and stolen cigarettes. As he walked past they crowded furtively into the shelter, seeking out the deeper shadows, careful not to look up at him as they moved. In the daytime he'd probably have recognised them all, but now, in the night, the only one he could be sure of was Jack Tatws, whose father owned a field of potatoes behind his house. Jack, he remembered, had once played the big xylophone in a harvest festival concert in the church, put on by the village primary school. They were the ones he always noticed, those ones whose fingers were not subtle enough for recorders or guitars, whose ears could not pick up a tune, and so instead were handed big sticks with felt heads and left to go about their asynchronous thumping like monkeys in a circus beating toy drums. He liked their solitary persistence, their frantic and smiling oblivion amongst rhythms and melodies that must have sounded to them as distant and unattainable as the planetary symphony conducted in the spheres.

He carried on up the hill, flanked by terraces, until he reached the brow, where he stopped to sit on a wall and rest his ankle. It was hurting quite badly now. Beside him was the local Spar shop and opposite it a large square building with a sharp triangular roof. It was called Bethania and had been a chapel until just after the war — when maybe the local people had begun to realise that they'd built a chapel or two too many, that they didn't have quite as many souls now to fill them, that their presence hadn't done too much to stop what had happened — but had now, after years of dereliction, been converted, optimistically, into holiday flats. Looking at it he wasn't sure whether he shouldn't feel a certain glimmer of satisfaction to see this evidence of the decline in Nonconformist fortunes; but, considering the paltry level of attendance in his church, he thought it best not to. Besides, he liked this building, whose bold grey stones had somehow managed to avoid the rash of pebble-dash that seemed to afflict every other house in the village; it made them appear older, more enduring, and in the daylight, if you looked closely, you could see the unmistakable swirl of fossils embedded in them. They made him wonder how ancient they actually were — pre-Cambrian, Ordovician, antediluvian (which put him on safer ground, theologically speaking)? They'd been dynamited, broken up and carted here in the wake of religious shifts and schisms; how the great rifts they'd witnessed — tectonic, geological — must have made these seem the merest trifles: ripples and tremors all.

A semi-circle of light appeared suddenly in front of the Spar's doorway, and into it stepped Mrs Evans, carrying a red cotton bag (she didn't use the plastic shop ones) out of which poked a magazine and a newspaper. The Reverend Morris leapt instantly to his feet, thinking there was still time to slip behind the shop and avoid the conversation that he knew was coming; but, though he had been contemplating the drift of continents, he realised that shifting himself had become quite difficult. Dragging his ankle behind him, he'd got no further than the edge of the wall before he heard her voice: "Well, hello Mr Morris, and what brings you out this evening?" There was no escaping now.

Mrs Evans was one of his many slightly elderly female parishioners, of whom there were so many that he sometimes wondered if Welsh women actually died at all, if instead they were granted some kind of afterlife in this world, where they could harass their vicars as far down the corridors of eternity as it was humanly possible to go. None of them, however, was quite so pertinacious and voluble as Mrs Evans. Through the cold wind that spun in circles around the street, lifting up sweet wrappers and swirling them up into the night past the flapping wires of the electricity poles, she began to deliver a long and wearying jeremiad. Its subject was the degenerate elements who were swamping the locality, and its single example seemed to be the presence, in one of Cucu's fields, of two new age types who lived in a caravan. Morris, nodding assent at what he took to be the correct intervals, looked down and watched as his hands began to turn red and then purple. He was used to this, although he still wondered sometimes what exactly the likes of Mrs Evans wanted from him. Was it just a captive (and by now frozen) ear? No, he knew it was more — there was always Mike Spar and Dylan Post just for that — knew how on one level what they wanted was for him to lock their insights into a Christian embrace, to rubber stamp their prejudices and grievances and fears with the imprimatur of holy authority, to assure them that the errant BT repairman would face the very highest justice, to make it plain that God himself looked extremely poorly upon the recent defacement of the bus shelter. And, in a better temper and on warmer days, he could understand this need. Judgements and apprehensions and frustrations were a lonely business, why shouldn't they seek out companionship, and His companionship at that? And he could understand as well the downward slant of much of these laments. He was old himself. What could be more natural than to see reflected in the world around you the evidence of that decay to which you yourself were subject, to view alteration through the lens of disintegration; why shouldn't eyes that were failing see failure? It was an anthropomorphic folly, of course, an almost profane equation, but it was instinct too, the same as any other animal's need to build a shelter around itself, where it could live, or die. What he couldn't understand, in Mrs Evans' case at least, were the particular snobberies that muddied these waters. Why should she single out two hippies who'd dragged a caravan into a field for her opprobrium and, at the same time, praise what that man Giles had done just above them, vandalising the old windmill — would no one allow these poor rocks to rest — turning it into some Disney-gothic monstrosity? What made the one seem like the wrinkles on her skin and the other like plastic surgery? By the time she'd finished he was despondent.

...the times we used to walk along the cliff tops, all the way from Penmon to Traeth Coch, past the old quarries at Caim and Dock, over Y Fedw and under Bwrdd Arthur, and down onto those wide sands that never were red. It used to seem like the longest journey ever made. And Nain would make sandwiches and barley water to provision us, enough to last us to the ends of the earth, and we'd carve boughs of hazel as swords and walking sticks, hacking our way through armies of nettles, bramble battalions. Do you remember passing the mad old man who lived in Maes y Mor, Glyn Ding-a-Ling, who skulked in his garden, waiting for us to steal his apples, and then rushed after us, as big as a Cyclops, waving his knotted cane above his head like a war club? Do you

remember sitting on the rocks of Chwalar Wen, looking hard at the skyline, seeing if we could see the outline of the Isle of Man and pretending we could see Ireland and you said it was America and I said nobody could see that far. I still wonder when all of this began to shrink for you, when the flurry of childish steps became the merest Brobdingnagian stride, when all those horizons we couldn't see became no more than the name on a one-way ticket, when this bounded circle of shore became the constraining hoop that you had to jump through, and then beyond. When did it all come to seem too little, and then not enough. Sometimes I think....

As she moved off down the pavement he watched as the wind pulled strands of greying hair out from under the edges of a woolen scarf that she had tied ever so carefully about her head.

* * * *

Gwynfor Garage's garage was at the top of the village, just beyond a football pitch where several sheep were huddled beneath a rusty pair of goalposts. It looked like a house, like any other of the houses that stood beside it, with their flecks of gravel — a mixture of myriad shades of grey — clinging to their walls, only its bottom floor had been turned into a wide door of corrugated metal that each morning slid open to reveal a bewildering array of twisted steel carcasses that seemed to have been there for so long that it was easy to imagine Gwynfor's had become some kind of automobiles' graveyard, a place where moribund motors, hearing their death rattle, crawled into so they might join the corroded bones of their forbears. Outside, on the forecourt, there were two petrol pumps, although these had been out of use for such an age that even amongst the whitest beards in the village there was still some debate as to whether there had ever been a time when they actually dispensed anything. Occasionally, particularly in the spring, visitors to the island, passing through the village, would stop their cars beside these pumps and wait for a small eternity until finally Gwynfor himself would shuffle out, responding to their requests for fuel with a baffled taciturnity, like a farmer who'd been asked the origin and purpose of the mouldering cromlechs in his field.

Reverend Morris leaned for a moment on one of the pumps, gathering thoughts which the wind had begun to scatter, smelling the coal smoke that careered down the roof slates towards him and then shuttled off along the street towards the dark fields beyond. He wondered why Gwynfor had called for him, what could be wrong with his wife? Over the years he had become used to making unusual house calls, whose purposes were as often as not only loosely contained within the purview of matters spiritual. In the past he had been the adjudicator in family conflicts, the comforter and advisor of pregnant, husbandless girls, the assuager of angry fathers, the rebuker of godless sons. Most often, in the days before GPs prescribed things for sadness, he had acted as a kind of doctor for the melancholy (the indigenous affliction that seeped through the streams here), an unofficial post requiring of him long hours in silent, stricken kitchens, where he tried his best to smooth over the inexplicability, the awkwardness, the sheer embarrassment of despair. Because so often there was no cause —

no skeleton falling out of the closet, no lowering of coffins, no note on the table and bloody mess in the bathroom — only a waking up to find that that same square of garden and bundle of bushes and rickety wooden fence that had sat outside your window all your life had suddenly become the most hopeless prospect in the entire world, a landscape sedimented with layer upon layer of futility and sorrow, as if everything you had ever lost, or never had, was fossilised in it. And afterwards the befuddled, stuporous immobility, as though you had sunk beneath thick, clammy oceans, with people's voices sounding weakly from a thousand fathoms above and you down here where the sunlight would never reach and the water clogged your lungs and the grey weeds wrapped themselves around your useless limbs. No cause, and when it happened how could you explain, and how could the rest of them understand. So they would call the Reverend Edward Morris, who would troop off through the rain on nights such as this, and try to make things a bit easier, a bit less extraordinary, as though only an exegete of miracles could drag it, gasping, into the cold light of day.

Looking up at the floral curtains on the second floor, lit up faintly from within, he hoped it would not be anything like this. In his memory there were rooms that felt infectious; places where the air made his skin prickle and whispered voices felt hot and humid like malarial breezes; wan figures crouched leper-like in corners. He felt too old now to be immune from it, as though all the antibodies of hope and belief and persistence that had shielded him once were drying up — thin, friable strands floating abandoned in his blood. He hoped it would not be this.

* * * *

Three knocks and the door was open. Gwynfor produced a grunt that passed for a greeting and led him through into the kitchen, where the two of them stood in a windless silence, Gwynfor looking down at the gleaming linoleum floor while Morris surveyed the walls. There was a picture of their son, Will, a giant of a boy, trapped uncomfortably in a school uniform that clung to his precociously bulging body, and beside it a tea cloth decorated with green hills and an Irish flag, inscribed with a proverb that ended with the line "May the wind always be at your back", which right now Morris very much wished to be the case. On the opposite wall there was a painting, although painting did not really describe it, it was more a tableau vivant, in which a huge waterfall cascaded from the edge of a forested plateau. The water itself seemed to be made out of ridged and striated white plastic, through which a sequence of lights glowed, ebbing downwards and crashing onto the rocks beneath. Morris watched it for some time, struck by how easily transfixed he was by this cheap and gaudy illusion of movement. It was a good few minutes before he looked down and realised that his clothes were covered in mud. Feeling embarrassed suddenly he tried making conversation with Gwynfor.

"Terrible weather we're having," he said.

"Yes," Gwynfor replied, darting out a faintly accusing look. Meanwhile, the mud was becoming an ever more insistent question and Morris was greatly relieved when Gwynfor finally asked it,

"You have a fall?"

"No, not really. Just a tumble." Gwynfor nodded his head.

And just at that moment, which was an even greater relief, Catrin walked into the room.

She arrived speaking, as though she had already begun warming up in the corridor outside. Small and squat, with an air of perpetual motion about her, she always gave the impression that she was half way through at least five or six separate conversations, which she was obliged to shift her attention quickly between, balancing them like a juggler.

"Well, Mr Morris, isn't it lovely to see you. Hasn't Gwynfor got you some tea yet, Duw, I'll get it myself then. What he does all day down in that garage I don't know. I was telling Mair today, I see these cars go in there but I never see them coming out. And she says it's the same with her Idris, going out on his tractor all day and her not seeing any difference in the fields afterwards, and I said no it's hard to tell what they're doing, and she says well it's probably better not to know, only they come back in the evening moaning like nobody's business. So how are you? What Gwynfor's up to dragging you out on a night like this is beyond me, really it is, and I told him not to, told him it wouldn't make a blind bit of difference, only be a trouble for you and everything, and there he goes and does it, doesn't he. And look at you, covered in mud, poor thing."

At which point she whisked his coat out of his hand and probably would have started washing it there and then if the kettle hadn't begun to boil. Morris always thought how apt it was that these two had married each other, how otherwise there would simply have not been enough room in the house for all their words.

Having expected the worst, Catrin's cheery volubility began to reassure him. Maybe they just wanted to donate something for the spring raffle? Whatever the case, he knew he wouldn't have to wait long to find out: Catrin would get to it soon enough. He was surprised how soon. As the table in front of him filled with cups and saucers, plates heaped with shortbread and biscuits, he listened to what he would never have expected: "And I said to him, there's no use in trying to stop me, I've made up my mind and that's that. I've made the arrangements: Angharad and her husband are expecting me and they've said I can live with them as long as I want because the house is too big for just the two of them anyway, although why they'd want a house that big in the first place I don't know, but they're cheaper in Spain I suppose so why not have one with four bedrooms instead of just the two. But no, he won't get it into his thick head that I'm leaving, and Esgob Mawr I've told him enough times that I am. So what does he do but go about trying to get everyone in the village to have a talk with me, like that was going to change anything. I've made up my mind and that's that and God almighty isn't going to persuade me otherwise."

The Reverend Morris didn't know what to say. But he had to say something. Gwynfor was looking utterly helpless, his shoulders slumping almost to the edge of the table, his face contorted with the effort to get out the words that wouldn't come — it was the one time in all his sixty years that he had something he really wanted to say, and he couldn't. So Morris said them: "But Catrin, this has been your home for forty years, and you've always lived in the village."

"That's what I've bloody well been trying to tell her!" Gwynfor gasped, the effort of it throwing him back into his chair. Catrin hardly blinked an eye.

"Well that's my point exactly Mr Morris, though you'd think it was rocket science the way it bounces off his bloody skull. I've been here for as long as I remember and one morning I just wake up and I'm thinking I'm not staying any more, I'm not going to sit around like one of those old buckets of rust downstairs, waiting till I'm nothing but dirt and dust. I don't have to. I'm thinking it's not like I'm some heap of stones stuck forever on the ground — I can get on a plane and go. I've life enough in me yet you know."

* * * *

...that at a certain point our vision somehow forked, like two roads splitting apart, and that you started wanting views that were horizontal, that unfolded sideways into space, when the only vistas here were vertical, slanting down into time, and those were mine. But what if I was wrong? What if all along it was me who wanted the wide horizon, to have prairies beneath my feet instead of graveyards, fields without walls, to walk as far as I wanted, without turning or veering, and not fall into the ocean. Because there are times now when the smallest crack in the clouds is enough to set my heart racing, when the feel of the wind on my back conjures continents, when the smallest raindrop on my window expands like the Pacific. And have you ever noticed how rock pools, when the tide is down, and the sea seems far away, look like the loneliest places in the world....

The night was dark and he was tired and his foot was hurting. Sitting down on a stone beside the road he looked into the blackness, unable to see anything, unable to move anywhere, not knowing how far away his home was.

Ynys

Spotting it seemed almost miraculous, a pretty piece of providence. Only I'd been trying hard the last few weeks not to react too strongly to things so I looked at it with equanimity, even though inside I could feel that uplift beneath the sternum, as though your stomach has been pumped with helium, and could feel the moisture welling somewhere behind my eyes. It's only a picture I told myself, trying to regulate pulses and heartbeats, breathing carefully, only a picture, and a fairly unremarkable one at that. But it was unmistakable. The black lines etched casually against a white background, forming a hill at first — out of which charcoal hawthorn trees grew and squiggled bundles of gorse — then moving inexorably upwards into the centre of the whiteness, gathering together there to create the outline of broken stones, forgotten walls. I didn't even walk into the gallery, didn't even look at the name of the painter or the title of the picture. All I needed to know I had known instantly, the first moment I set eyes on it through the window. I quickly gave it colour, fleshed it out into springtime, making the gorse flower yellow and the hill blossom green, spreading blue where the sea should have been and a distant, dusky verdure on the undrawn haunt of eagles that would have been on the horizon. I gave the stones texture, layer on layer of flaking whitewash, blotches of spongy lichen, patches of crumbling grey. And then I carried the restored image of it with me for the whole day, which felt like the longest time I'd held onto anything for ages.

That night I dreamt of islands. Not one in particular, not mine specifically, but scattered, endless archipelagos; some with sand and coral reefs, some with sheer cliffs and thumping surf, some flat and arid, every type of island you could imagine. In the dream I was afraid of water and floated uneasily through the air above a wide ocean, searching for the islands, filled with a terrible anxiety that I would not reach the next one. When I woke it took a while for me to alight properly on my bed. I could hear the sound of cars rushing past down the A40 and the old Irish woman who lived in the flat above mine pissing, an incongruously loud and vigorous cascade — belying her thin and fragile frame — that echoed through the whole room. "It's your bladder that goes first," I remembered my uncle Emlyn telling me in The Dragon once, before scuttling off to the toilet. Evidently not everybody's. He told me a good deal more that night. Told me that they were selling Pen y Mor because there was nothing they could do with it, now that my auntie, his sister, was dead and there was nobody to live in it. Besides, he told me, all beer and money-drunk as he was, they'd make a packet from it and I'd get my share, "Don't you worry lad." And now some actress, who plays a barmaid in a Sunday drama, set in some quirky but endearing village (Irish or Scottish naturally — it's got to be romantic hasn't it) owns the house I grew up in, slumming it in

Wales for a few months a year — a rural interlude to recover from the labour of filming a rural interlude. And meanwhile I am left here, in unleafy Acton, with a good job and lots of prospects, listening to a toilet flush, outraged at my own dispossession.

* * * *

My great, great grandfather, Tudur ap Tudur built that house. I think he was a pirate. When I was a boy I desperately hoped he had been. I still do. It all made sense. My auntie said he had been a merchant, which I've always suspected was a euphemism, because why would any merchant build a cottage on a lonely cliff top — not for the view, certainly. Besides, there was proof enough on the ground: caves where Jack Bach and Dewi Tew and I played as children and found brass buckles and a candlestick; ruined stone sheds, hidden in the willow shrubs, where they must have stored their booty. Plus our side of the island had a pirate pedigree, long family lines of wreckers and plunderers who set lights on the cliff tops to guide the ships of unwitting visitors onto the rocks. Now the visitors buy their houses.

Adding to his lustre, in my eyes definitely, Tudur ap Tudur the pirate married a witch. My auntie never mentioned it, but Bachie's nain did once, when I went around there for tea. We were eating baked beans and she was buttering bread and then out it slipped. Bachie's mother told her not to *siarad gwirion*, but I was delighted. It explained a lot of things, chief among them the shock of red hair on my head. You see hundreds of years ago, or so the story goes, two boats drifted ashore on the sands of a beach not more than two miles down the coast from my house. The boat carried a quite extraordinary, and flamy-haired collection of flotsam. The men became expert smugglers, slipping along the island's coasts like shadows, carrying magic flies in their cravats, which, if the men were cornered, would buzz into the air and blind their pursuers. The women made a great trade in curses, paid in equal measure to either cast or withhold them. The beach is still called Traeth Coch, and, if you walk up to the village behind it, you will find it swarming with redheads and black cats. So, seeing he was a man with a substantial, if erratic income, and had just built himself a house, it was probably the most natural thing in the world for Tudur to make the short stroll down the coast to claim one of these poison-tongued enchantresses as his prize. And there must have been, I'm sure, all manner of side benefits to this union: many a customs man who found himself tossed helplessly around by a mysterious, mid-July squall, or woke up to find the hair on his head fallen onto his pillow. But however it came to pass, there is no refuting that Siani Bwt became his wife, and that it is to her I owe the copper coronet that crowns my skull.

After Tudur and Siani, my family suffered a great decline into respectability. My great grandfather disgraced himself by becoming a cobbler. Dafydd ap Tudur, stitching brogues after his Dad had robbed barques — I shudder to think of it. Then came my taid, who was dead before I was born. He spurned shoes, but loved bread, and built a bakery in the village, and then went and fell ingloriously off a boat at Dunkirk, drowning in the English

Channel. How poor Tudur must have flinched, up there in pirate heaven. But before he gave up his ghost to Saxon waters, my taid had laid down the rickety foundations of my future. First he gave me a father (and an uncle and auntie too, which was lucky and unlucky I suppose) and then he gave me a name.

I don't know the ins and outs of how it happened, but somewhere in the past there is a recruitment centre — maybe in Wrexham, maybe Caernarfon — with a desk and a piece of paper in the corner. In front of it stands my taid, dressed in his Sunday best, the flour combed carefully out of his hair, and behind it some English officers, looking suspiciously down at the ink that is drying beneath their noses. The name that ink has shaped is Alun ap Dafydd, and they don't like it, not one bit. It must have been the ap, which in those paranoid days probably seemed almightily dubious and foreign, a mere stone's throw from von. But whatever their motivations, by the time that piece of paper found its way into the intransigent tangle of officialdom, my taid had become Alun Davies, which is what he remained for the next, and last, year of his life. Now since it was this name that my nain saw typed on the telegraph, which would be the last official mention of her husband, the last moment he existed on government paper, it was the name she gave to her newly born son, my father, who in turn passed it on to me.

If it hadn't been for some unruly cells, a bottle of whiskey, and a ram, it would not have been the only thing he passed on to me. Sometimes I think old Tudur must have used up our family luck, squandered it recklessly on the high seas and left all of us lubbers who came after him impoverished, lugging around empty coffers of fortune. Because what else can explain the ill-starred fates of his progeny? You see my taid was not the first to die before his time. First there was his sister's husband, a Mr Edward Edwards, who, before even the war had time to kill him, managed to fall off the edge of his roof and to keep on falling, right off the edge of this world. And then there was my mother. I was three years old when it began. There was a headache, and then a trip to the hospital, and then another trip to the hospital, and then she didn't come home and there were visitors everywhere in the house. I was four years old when it ended. We took her to the family lot, where my auntie pointed out my other relatives. Then, six months later, my father. We lived in the bakery back then — we let Taid's widowed sister live in Pen y Mor, where she could grow vegetables in the garden to keep her occupied — and after mum went my father burnt the bread and drank as much as he could. One night he drank a whole bottle of whiskey and went out somewhere in the bakery van. The next morning my uncle was in the kitchen, talking to a policeman, who said my father must had swerved suddenly to avoid hitting something on the road — his money was on Cucu's old ram, Billy, who liked eating the ivy off the walls. This time when we went to the lot I knew where my relatives were. Afterwards my auntie took me back to Pen y Mor, where she brought me up. My uncle sold the bakery.

When I die, and they take me to the lot, I want my whole and proper name restored on my gravestone: Alun ap Alun ap Alun ap Dafydd ap Tudur ap Tudur.

Once upon a time we were overweeningly proud of our genealogies. We paid poets to recite them. We listened attentively, pleased to have venerable pasts, and then that's all we had.

* * * *

I say almost miraculous because for the last month I had thought of little else. Before then I suppose I'd been quite happy, though given over to periods of inexplicable moroseness, that baffled and annoyed my friends. During one of these attacks of spleen, or melancholy, or whatever you might call it, as I sat slumped and taciturn in a noisy pub, my friend's girlfriend — an indomitably cheerful Australian, assigned to me, I'm sure, to wear down my defiant moodiness — asked me if I was ever homesick. Now I know it sounds strange, but none of my friends had ever asked me this before. I suppose it never occurred to them. And why would it? When you live in London, and have come from Wales, I think they assume you are grateful, relieved even. I mean it's not like you've come from America or Australia or Kazakhstan, some *real* country that you might actually miss. Besides, I have lived here for almost a decade, ever since I arrived to go to university, and have not been back for five years, ever since my uncle sold my house. So when she asked me this I was not really certain what to say, yet somehow the question itself made me feel suddenly better. I laughed and told her that where I came from you were homesick even when you were at home. She laughed as well, but I hadn't meant it as a joke.

However, these saturnine intervals apart, for the most part I was pleased enough. I wasn't a pirate, which was disappointing, but I worked for a merchant bank — the next best thing I suppose. I didn't have a cottage on the cliff tops, but I had a flat of my own. And, of course, I was young and in the middle of things, where everything happened. Perhaps I should have been grateful, perhaps I was. I thought I was in love too, if I haven't mentioned that already.

I met her three years ago. She worked for a magazine, writing articles about films and music. She had been born in London but was half-Cuban, tall and dark, with lovely, crooked white teeth. I liked the fact that some part of her was from an island. I liked to think that detachment ran mutually through our blood, that we were somehow adrift together. But she never talked about her island and when I look back now I don't think it ever interested her that much, nor mine for that matter. They were just dots in the sea, parts of the puzzle that had brought us here, points of transit on a map of chance and coincidence. And, at first, I think I fell in love with this easy mobility. I wanted desperately to believe, with her, that homes were something you created, that you pieced together out of where you happened to be, and so everything you needed and loved you carried with you. There were no drizzly lots in her world, pieces of earth where her dead family lived and could not be moved from, and for the two years I was with her there were none in mine.

My strongest memories of her are mostly fragments from old movies and songs. Jimmy Stewart standing beside the pool in The Philadelphia Story. Billie Holliday singing Day In, Day Out. The dashing feet of Gene Kelly on the streets of MGM Paris. They were her favourite things, all a part of the airy firmament on which she grounded herself. She introduced them to me like relatives, and, like any good boyfriend, I pretended to like them as much as she did. Getting to know her was like watching a building being slowly built; seeing the process whereby, piece by piece, she had constructed her own inheritance, herself. And I was happy sharing it, I really was. For those years I was a part of it, woven into its very fabric, and everything that had come before was like an anchor cast into the ocean.

I still don't know when exactly my newfound, giddy freedom turned into anxiety and dislocation. I try to visualise it as a particular moment, a scene: the two of us together in a restaurant, her getting up to go, a staged glimmer of despondency about my eyes, an intimation of lostness, a comforting look from the waiter. But it wasn't like that, it never is. Looking back I cannot find a beginning, just as now I cannot really see an ending. It was such a subtle transformation, no more than a flicker on the edges of the screen, but afterwards the mobility that I loved in her had become, ineluctably, the fear that I would lose her, that she would pack herself up again and be gone as easily as she had alighted. I felt her absence creeping around each corner. It polluted everything, tainted every moment with departure, and then of course she did leave. I could have stopped her, I could have made her stay, but I thought it was better this way, that at least I would not have to suffer the agony of waiting anymore. Besides, neither of us walked into any distant sunsets or strode down the stairs into a stormy night. Every few months or so there would be a phone call, and one or the other of us would traipse off across the city and into the other's bed. I remember these journeys — the shudder of the underground, the eerie passing of night-time faces, pavements shining under orange lamps — but I am not certain what impelled them, whether it was hope, or lust, or loneliness, or sheer boredom. Maybe it was all of them, maybe this is just love's residue — the detritus we leave behind in parting. I wish now that that was all I'd left behind.

* * * *

The last of these nights was three months ago. Six weeks later she called to tell me she was pregnant — at first I thought she meant by someone else. There was no question what would happen. We waited together for two weeks. The night before it she couldn't sleep and tried to touch me. I flinched and turned away, watching through her window as whispering cars ebbed away into a wet, asphalt darkness that lapped against the glass. I didn't want the light to come. The next morning we got into a cab and drove west, that is all I remember, that it was far into the west, past Chiswick and Richmond, until there were trees and big gardens. And then it was over, more quickly then I had imagined. I stayed that night and in the morning she told me to leave, she told me not to call again, she said that this was the last time and I already knew it was.

In my room in Pen y Mor there is a window. It looks up from the sea and across the fields towards a hill where a lonely tower stands, an island on an island. Since that day I have thought about nothing else. That picture could have been my window frame; when I saw it first I half thought it was — that all the years had crumbled backwards and left a four year old boy looking out for the first time on all that was left to him. I told her once about my house and before I knew it there were tears on my face. I said I was ashamed I had lost it, that it felt like because of losing it I had lost everything, that now I came from nowhere. And she put her arm around my shoulders and smiled and said I shouldn't worry so much about it, that all of us are from somewhere else, if you go far back enough, that it's where we've got to that counts, that really matters. But if that is true then why haven't I got far enough away to leave this behind, why can't I give it up and start again from where I am.

First I lost a house because I had no father to keep it for me, now I have lost the child I should have bequeathed it to. So how much further must I go, how much more must I give away? How much must you lose before you realise that one patch of ground, one piece of sky, one hill, one tower, mean everything?

Glossary

nain — grandmother (north Wales)
Sais — English person
taid — grandfather (north Wales)
Gruffydd Felin — Gruffydd the Mill
Dewi Tew — Fat Dewi
Jach Bach — Little Jack
Traeth Coch — Red Beach
ynys — island
ap — son of
siarad gwirion — talk daft